Join Hercules on all of his heroic journeys . . .

### By the Sword
Hercules' smashing debut! Marauders have stolen Zeus's magical sword of fire. It's up to Hercules to recover it—but someone very powerful has plans for the sacred blade. *And* for Hercules!

### Serpent's Shadow
A small village calls on Hercules and Iolaus to battle a deadly sea monster. But when they discover the sea monster is only part of a trap set by Hera, can even Hercules' great strength save them?

*All-new, original adventures!*

BE SURE NOT TO MISS BOULEVARD'S ALL-NEW SERIES STARRING

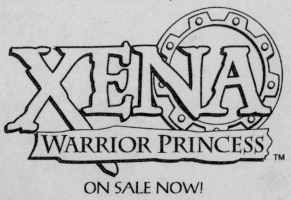

### ON SALE NOW!

# HERCULES
## THE LEGENDARY JOURNEYS™

# THE EYE
# OF THE RAM

A novel by Timothy Boggs
based on the Universal television series
created by Christian Williams

**Executive Producers Sam Raimi
and Robert Tapert**

BOULEVARD BOOKS, NEW YORK

HERCULES: THE LEGENDARY JOURNEYS: THE EYE OF THE RAM

A novel by Timothy Boggs, based on the Universal television series
HERCULES: THE LEGENDARY JOURNEYS, created by Christian Williams.

HERCULES: THE LEGENDARY JOURNEYS ™ & © 1997 MCA Television
Limited. All rights reserved. Licensed by MCA/Universal
Merchandising, Inc.
A Boulevard Book / published by arrangement with
MCA Publishing Rights, a Division of MCA, Inc.

PRINTING HISTORY
Boulevard edition / February 1997

The Putnam Berkley World Wide Web site address is
http://www.berkley.com/berkley

Make sure to check out *PB Plug*, the science fiction/fantasy newsletter,
at http://www.pbplug.com

ISBN: 1-57297-224-6

BOULEVARD
Boulevard Books are published by The Berkley Publishing Group,
200 Madison Avenue, New York, New York 10016.
BOULEVARD and its logo are trademarks
belonging to Berkley Publishing Corporation.

PRINTED IN THE UNITED STATES OF AMERICA

10  9  8  7  6  5  4  3  2  1

For Mighty Wes,
a Hercules in his own right,
and a mean hand with a mean horn;

and Josh the Silent,
whose hobby is losing hubcaps,
and bloody good at it he is, too.

# THE EYE
# OF THE RAM

# 1

Agatra was not the most beautiful woman in the world.

In fact, as local song and story have it, the men of the village of Nevila were hard-pressed to call her a woman at all. The only reason they did so was out of an acute sense of self-preservation. Those same local songs and stories have recorded instances of noses being skewered, hair being plucked by the strand from beards and scalps, and worse atrocities, just because a man forgot to say, "Morning there, Agatra, you're looking lovely today."

For a man, life in Nevila was just one damn thing after another.

The women, on the other hand, understood Agatra fairly well; and while they certainly didn't condone the plucking and the skewering most of the time, they knew they often felt that way themselves—whenever things weren't going right, nothing fit, their hair wouldn't obey the brush or the comb, and the kids had turned into demonic spawn overnight.

There was, therefore, a certain kinship between the Nevilian women and Agatra, a bond that often saw a woman climb the wooded hillside in order to have a long heart-to-heart with her friend. Sometimes the woman returned red-eyed from sobbing, but serene and ready to move on; sometimes the woman returned without having visibly received any help at all; and once in a great while, the woman returned with iron in her spine and ice in her eyes, which was when the men knew the skewering and plucking were about to begin.

Late one morning a woman named Peyra made the climb.

There was no path, no trail; there were no signposts.

The women of Nevila knew the way by instinct.

Peyra was young and slender, her dark brown hair falling in thick waves to the center of her back and held away from her matching eyes by a wide red band. By her clothes it was clear she wasn't wealthy, nor was she ragged. Around her waist was a narrow leather belt from which hung a bulging pouch.

She made her way quickly through the widely spaced, high-crowned trees, oblivious to the blue sky, the gentle warm breeze, and the profusion of wildflowers that would have, on another occasion, made her laugh with the sheer joy of such a splendid display.

Eventually she reached a broad clearing. There were no flowers here, and the grass didn't dare grow very high. The slope rose precipitously at the back, and in its solid rock face was the mouth of a cave flanked by two twisted, stunted, virtually leafless trees that seemed as old as the hill itself.

Peyra hesitated as she stepped into the open. Maybe this wasn't such a good idea. Maybe she should go farther afield, to one of the cities, to find what she needed. They were rumored to have anything a person could possibly want, natural or otherwise.

But she didn't know the cities, and she did know Agatra.

There was no one else who could help her.

Nervously she brushed her hands over her hair, smoothed the skirt of her dress, adjusted her belt, and patted her cheeks and brow to rid them of possible unseemly perspiration.

"Well, Zeus and beanpods," a voice called harshly, "are you going to stand there all day?"

Peyra smiled.

Agatra was home.

To the right of the cave's entrance was a boulder whose flat top had been smooth by the rump of many a visitor. It was just the height of a chair, and Peyra sat there comfortably, facing the cave. She couldn't see inside. Even when the sun was at its brightest and its light filled the clearing, an inch inside the cave there appeared to be no light at all.

Once settled, she said, "Good afternoon, Agatra. I have a problem."

"Of course you do. Nobody ever visits me otherwise. Nobody ever comes along just for the hell of it, do they? Bring me a pie, a dumpling, a little stew in the winter when my bones are creaking. No, they only come when they have a problem. I could be lying here, dying, falling apart, ants and spiders dividing me up for rations, and nobody would know it. Never write, never call out a greeting on the way by.''

Peyra's smile broadened.

She was in luck.

Agatra was in a good mood.

''So, dearie, what can I do for you?''

Peyra wasn't sure how to begin. In the first place, listening to that rasping voice for any length of time made her want to clear her throat, cough, or beg for a drink of water. But if she did, Agatra would be insulted and force her to leave. In the second place, if she didn't word her problem correctly, Agatra might do something terrible, like plucking or skewering, neither of which were appropriate in this case.

''A man, right?'' Agatra said in as solicitous a tone as that voice ever got.

Peyra shifted, and patted the pouch resting in her lap. ''Well, yes. Sort of. My husband, actually.''

''Ah. Young . . . Garus, am I right?''

Peyra nodded sadly.

''Oh my, I do hope he's all right.''

Peyra shook her head, and scowled at a sudden sting of tears. She had promised herself she wouldn't do this. Agatra hated it.

''I hate that,'' Agatra snapped. ''Stop it at once.''

The stinging vanished.

''Now. Start at the beginning, dearie. I've got plenty of time. I always have plenty of time. Nothing else to do. Nobody here but you and me. Nobody's ever here. I'm all alone. In the dark. Just me. And a cockeyed spider.''

Peyra couldn't help it; she giggled.

Agatra laughed. At least, Peyra thought it was a laugh. It sounded like someone coughing her way along the high road to an urgent appointment with Hades. Whatever it was, however, it made Peyra feel better already.

''Well,'' she began, staring at the worn grass at her feet, ''we were in Hyanth, Garus and I were. Visiting, you know?''

''No,'' Agatra grumbled sourly. ''I wouldn't know.''

Peyra ignored her. ''We were looking for new cloth, something not seen around here often, and Hyanth, being on the crossroads, sometimes has things like that. For our shop, you know? Garus, he always looks for the bright stuff, the really make-your-eyes-close bright stuff. I myself was after something a little more subtle.''

''Like blood red?''

''Yeah. It kind of makes a fashion statement, you know what I mean?''

''Haven't a clue, dearie.''

''Oh.'' Peyra could sense the impatience, closed her eyes briefly, and patted the pouch again. ''Anyway, our second day we heard there were going to be some performers in the square, so instead of coming home like we planned, we decided to stay another night and have a look.''

''Your idea,'' Agatra said. ''Not his.''

5

Peyra nodded, and felt the stinging again. "Yes."

"Something happened."

"Yes."

"Something terrible."

"Yes."

"You going to tell me or do I have to guess?"

Peyra couldn't stop the tears this time, and she turned her head away in embarrassment, trying to dry them with the backs of her hands and her sleeves. Her sleeves got soaked, and the tears kept falling.

A noise then, like the gentle scraping of powerful, and really sharp, claws on the ground. Peyra couldn't believe it, and whirled just as Agatra stepped out of her cave.

Down in the village, and in the fields, and in the forest, and along the wide stream that ran past the village, every man froze in terror and inexplicable guilt.

In the trees around the clearing, the birds couldn't decide whether to flee or freeze, and one was so indecisive he fell off his branch.

To the left of the cave's entrance, opposite the rock on which Peyra sat, was a fallen tree whose bark, in places, had been rubbed off to the dark gray wood beneath and pocked with deep holes. Agatra didn't like the rock because she kept sliding off; she liked the tree because her talons could take better hold.

For good reason, Agatra was not the most beautiful woman in the world.

She was a Harpy.

It took a while for Agatra to settle herself on her perch. Unlike most of her kind, she was on the plump side, and while she insisted she only looked that way because her wings refused to lie straight, not even the men were fooled into thinking she was svelte.

And while her body resembled a sated, gluttonous robin after a particularly wonderful spring, her neck and head were those of a woman who had seen far too many springs slip away behind her. Her wrinkles were legendary, her thinning hair gray and in a sloppy braid around her crown, and not even her closest kin talked about the wattles.

Not if they didn't want to be plucked and skewered. And gutted.

Her eyes, however, were amazing. Large, slightly tilted at the corners, and of a blue that changed hue with every change of her mood. Which meant that most of the time they were ice or the center of a flame; now, however, they were warm, the color of a perfect summer morning.

"He dead?" she asked, clasping her hands in front of her. She may have been old, but her arms were thick enough to fell a tree with a single blow.

"No," Peyra sobbed. "Oh, Agatra, he's a frog!"

Agatra harrumphed. "Of course he's a toad, dearie. He's a man, isn't he?"

Peyra blinked. "No."

The Harpy sighed. "I know he's your husband, child, but be honest with yourself—he's still a man."

7

"No." Peyra reached into the pouch. "I meant what I said." She held out her palm. "He's a frog!"

Agatra looked, squinted, frowned, and nodded. "Be damned, you're right. He *is* a frog. Ugly, too. Who ever heard of a yellow frog?"

Frogs, when faced with a predatorial bird the size of a Harpy, either dove instantly into whatever water happened to be around and held their breath for several days, or they froze. Men, when faced with Agatra, froze. Men who used to be men but now were frogs did the only thing they could do—they rolled onto their backs and played dead.

Agatra looked at the frog lying on its back in Peyra's hand, looked at Peyra, and said, "I think, dearie, you'd better explain."

Then her stomach rumbled, and the frog may or may not have quivered a little.

The Harpy cleared her throat. "Sorry. Haven't had lunch yet."

Sensing the possibilities, Peyra hastily slipped her husband back into the pouch, composed herself, and said, "Well, it all started with this man who said he could pull a dinar out of a little boy's ear."

# 2

Sometimes even the best of days were spoiled by the ominous, and not always coherent, muttering of signs and portents.

A gentle sun and an eye-pleasing blue sky could be marred by the dark shadow of a circling hawk, a hunting eagle, or a vulture on its way to claim carrion for its own.

A comfortable breeze that caused the leaves to whisper and the grass to stir could carry on its back the muffled cough of a thief lurking in a thicket, or the rustle of a wolf making its way toward unsuspecting prey, or the smell of a flower that had no business blossoming in that season.

The shadows under a tree could, to the ordinary man, be nothing more than shadows; but to an extraordinary man, they could be subtle signals of approaching doom.

Hercules did not consider himself to be an extraordinary man.

That he was strong and powerful could not be

argued, but that was because he was a son of Zeus, not because of any weight training he had done other than tossing a few bad guys around. Neither did he think he was particularly ugly—or particularly handsome, for that matter—and he was therefore constantly surprised when women were drawn to him without even knowing his name. He didn't complain; he was just surprised.

And the gods certainly knew he wasn't the luckiest of men.

Consider the afternoon.

Originally he had intended to head up to Thrace, a place he hadn't visited in quite a while. Enjoy life without the hassles. Sleep. Eat. Hunt. Fish.

In other words, relax.

Adventures, unfortunately, kept getting in his way, and by the time he was free to return to the plan, he realized that it would be close to winter before he reached his destination. That meant tromping around a bunch of bare rocky mountains being pummeled by heavy snows, and strong winds cold enough to freeze the snakes off a gorgon.

Not even remotely his idea of proper relaxation.

His alternate plan, conceived just this morning, had been to drift south and west, visit a few friends, put his feet up and let the days slip by without once having to stop a war or unseat a dictator or save someone from someone else determined to end the first someone's life for purely selfish reasons.

All in all, it was a good notion.

Signs and portents had no place in it.

When they elbowed their way in anyway, he

couldn't help but wonder if maybe it wasn't time to put the always available emergency plan into action: find a deep cave, furnish it, roll a huge rock in front of it, and sit there for a few weeks, enjoying the peace, the dark, and the distinct absence of adventure.

The problem was—aside from the fact that there wasn't a cave handy—he wasn't the kind of man who could ignore those signs. And portents.

He sighed deeply—and loudly, in case anyone was listening and wanted to give him some pity— in resignation.

At first he wasn't sure he had heard anything at all.

Strolling through the lightly wooded forest had been uneventful thus far. Birds sang, tiny critters scuttled, the breeze blew, the sun warmed him, the road was clear and well marked, and he was at peace.

Until he thought he caught the sound of clanking metal.

A slight frown while he listened, a quick shake of his head when he decided he had been mistaken, and a complete rejection of the sound as a sign were all he needed to continue on his way.

Until he heard it again.

That was the problem with lightly wooded forests: sound carried. Especially the kind he didn't particularly want to hear.

When he heard it a third time, coupled with what could only be someone yelping in pain, he broke into a swift trot that quickly brought him around a bend in the road.

Another problem with lightly wooded forests was that you could see things in the distance.

In this case, two of the large, brightly decorated covered wagons the Athenians called caravans, each drawn by a pair of decidedly unhappy horses. On the one closest to him a man stood at the opening in back, swinging a short staff at a pair of men who, unfairly, were swinging long swords back. Beyond it, a second pair of men seemed to be trying to kick at something hidden under the caravan's bed.

The four thieves were hindered by a number of things, not the least of which was the horses, who reared, shied, sidestepped, and otherwise caused the heavy caravans to lurch and jerk, thus spoiling the aims of all involved.

For the briefest of moments Hercules thought the travelers would prevail. Until the horses hitched to the second vehicle decided to bolt. They couldn't, but the abrupt forward movement was enough to pitch the man in back to the ground.

The thieves cried out in triumph.

Hercules sprinted up the road, reaching the melee just as the fallen man raised his staff to block a blow and found it sliced rather neatly in half.

"Ha!" said one of the thieves.

"Help!" the fallen man cried.

"Sure," Hercules said.

The two thieves whirled, gaped, and might well have chosen a hasty retreat had not Hercules decided not to give them a choice. He grabbed one under the chin, heaved him off his feet, and pitched him into a nearby bush which, by the sound of the landing, was somewhat thorned. The second used the interlude to stab at Hercules' stomach. The trouble was, the stomach wasn't there when he finished his lunge, and he looked up pleadingly beneath a thick mop of curly hair just before he, too, was given flight.

The fallen merchant gasped his thanks.

Hercules nodded and hurried to the front wagon, where the remaining thieves were still kicking at a bundle of clothing huddled behind one tall wheel.

The clothing yelped.

The thieves laughed.

Hercules cleared his throat.

The thieves stopped laughing, turned, and one of them snarled, "Who are you?"—even as he drew a dagger from his belt.

Hercules spread his arms to prove not only that he was not carrying a weapon, but that his arms were considerably thicker, and stronger, than the thief's.

It was a silent warning.

The thief looked at his partner and grinned as if to suggest that this had turned out to be more fun than they had planned. The grin slipped away, however, when he noticed his partner backing away. "What's the matter with you, Chicus?" he demanded.

Chicus pointed a trembling finger. "I know him, Sid, I know him."

"So introduce us, dear brother," Sid answered with a nasty laugh, and a nastier wave of his dagger.

**13**

The second thief swallowed hard. "That's . . ." He paled. "It's . . ."

"Hercules," Hercules offered calmly.

Chicus nodded, blinked, and probably would have escaped into the woods had he not, in spinning around to flee, slammed into the high rear wheel and fallen flat on his back.

Sid, who was gap-toothed with a broad black mustache, then uttered a word which, in mixed company, would have probably gotten him lynched, and decided that flight was perhaps the wisest of choices after all.

It was, although probably not the kind of flight he had hoped for, as Hercules snared him by belt and scruff, hoisted him overhead, and tossed him easily into the two men near the second caravan, who had huddled together in an effort to come up with a plan to help their friends, and pluck out a few thorns.

The three went down in a symphony of grunts and moans, one that changed quickly to "Hey, knock it off!" and at least one "Yike!" when the merchant began to flail at them with his half-staff.

It wasn't long before they ran-stumbled into the woods, soon followed by their recovered partner.

Once the thieves were gone and clearly not about to return, Hercules shook his head in disappointment. Men like that were giving thievery a bad name. And they were brothers, too.

The merchant, puffing a bit, leaned heavily against the wagon's gate. "Thanks," he managed to say.

Hercules shrugged modestly. "My pleasure. Are you all right?"

"I think so, yes. More surprised than anything. They were hiding, you see. We weren't prepared." His expression hardened. "Should have been, though. After all this, we should have known it would happen."

Hercules didn't understand, and didn't pursue it. Utterances like that, when questioned, were the kind that almost always got him into predicaments. Instead, he took a step back and stared at the wagon.

Both vehicles were of a variety he had seen only a few times before. Each bed was enclosed by thin walls and a rounded roof. The walls were aswirl with painted flowers, images of gymnasts, tongues of fire, what might have been a roaring beast, and curlicues that ran like vines around the edges.

"Here," the merchant said, beckoning.

Hercules looked in the back.

It was crammed with at least a dozen large chests, each wrapped in chains.

He whistled silently. "So what is it? Gold? Silver?"

The merchant shook his head with a laugh. "I wish. No, friend, they're props and costumes."

"Yours?"

The man grunted. "Gods, no. The wagons are the only things that belong to me."

"You're not in charge?"

"Bite your tongue, sir, bite your tongue." He held out a hand in greeting. "My name is Flovi. Flovi Zigfalius."

Hercules gripped the offered hand, noting as he did that the man was a lot stronger than he looked.

Flovi was nearly as tall as he, and obviously lean despite the flowing brown robe he wore. His face was dark and lined, like that of a man who spent a great deal of time in the sun; it was marked by large gray eyes and a thick gray mustache that drooped past the corners of his mouth.

Hercules gestured toward the caravan. "I still don't get it."

Flovi opened his mouth to answer and groaned softly instead. Hercules caught him as he sagged against the gate, and eased him to the ground.

"Sorry," the man said, wincing. "I guess they caught me, after all."

Hercules spotted the rent in the cloth first. It was under the man's left arm, and he could see the faint stain of fresh blood. Flovi hissed when Hercules separated the tear, fearing the worst and puffing out a relieved breath when he saw that the gash was shallow, more ugly than lethal.

"Nothing serious," he announced.

"Worse luck," Flovi muttered.

Under the man's direction Hercules found a cloth in the wagon, tore them into manageable strips, and dipped it into a barrel of water lashed to the wagon's side. After cleansing the wound, he bound it snugly and helped Flovi back to his feet.

Another groan made him frown. "Are you sure you're all right?"

Flovi sighed. "That wasn't me."

Which was when Hercules finally remembered the bundle that had yelped when the thieves kicked it.

Rolling his eyes in disgust for forgetting, he re-

16

turned to the lead wagon, hunkered down, and looked under it. "Are you all right, friend?"

The bundle shifted, and a muffled voice said, "I'm dying. Dying, and nobody cares."

Hercules' eyes widened.

No, he thought, leaning back and shaking his head in dismay; please, gods, no.

He poked the bundle.

The bundle moaned.

Flovi came up behind him and said, "We could leave him there and nobody'd be any the wiser."

"Traitor," the bundle snapped. "After all I've done for you."

Flovi checked the area of his wound. "Oh, yeah, I forgot."

Hercules stood and nudged the bundle with his foot. "Get up. You're not hurt."

"I'm not?" the bundle exclaimed indignantly. "How can you say I'm not hurt? I could . . . I could be . . ."

The bundle rolled out from under the wagon, shook itself until it resolved into a man wearing a robe bright enough to blind the sun, and held out a hand that Hercules grabbed in order to yank the man to his feet.

He was modestly short, gently round in face and body; his hair began a third of the way back on his scalp in tight white curls and waves that darkened to brown by his ears and neck. His beard was short as well, and of the brown his hair probably once had been.

Almost immediately, his pained frown was replaced by a delighted smile.

"Hercules!" he cried, flinging his arms joyfully around him. "Hercules, what a wonderful, fortuitous, delightful surprise!"

Hercules patted the man on the back gingerly.

Signs and portents.

Maybe it wasn't too late to find that cave.

"Hello, Salmoneus," he said resignedly. "What have you gotten yourself into this time?"

# 3

The caravans moved slowly along the hard-packed road. The horses bobbed their heads in time to the pace, their tails every so often flicking pesky insects from their rumps. Glimpses of farmland could be seen to the right, in the far distance. A solid log bridge stretched over a wide rushing stream speckled with shade from overhanging trees.

From the driver's seat on the trailing wagon, Flovi entertained the woodland with songs that ranged from bawdy to mawkish. He had a wonderfully smooth baritone, the only fault being an occasional lapse in his ability to find the right note. His method to correct that fault was simple, get close enough, pounce, and pound it into shape.

The horses' ears twitched spastically at the result.

"All day," Salmoneus grumbled, glumly staring at the reins in his hands. "I hear that all day."

"I've heard worse," Hercules said just as a high note ricocheted off the scale. He winced. "Okay, maybe not."

"All day. All . . . day."

Hercules grinned, stretched, and told himself he ought to be grateful for the ride. Walking everywhere kept him in shape, allowed him to see things he might not ordinarily see, but as strong as they were, his legs didn't always appreciate the constant labor.

On the other hand, the ride was with Salmoneus.

That could only mean one thing, and he didn't want to dwell on it because it would only upset him.

Salmoneus was . . . different.

For as long as Hercules had known him, the man had never failed to be embroiled in some manner of controversy or outright mayhem. Not that he was a brawler or a warrior or a drunkard. Far from it. Salmoneus was one of the most gentle men Hercules had ever met.

The problem was his mind.

It never stopped working.

Ever.

As far as he could tell, Salmoneus' dream was to become the richest man in the world. It had nothing to do with power; it had everything to do with the usually cheerful man's constant search for that which had never existed before. Idea's, schemes, inventions—they came to him by the dozens, and Hercules didn't think Salmoneus ever turned one away, no matter how outlandish.

During one of their first meetings, Salmoneus had decided he could turn a fast dinar by following Hercules around and writing down everything he said and did. He called the project a celebrity biography, which, when copied in sufficient quantity, would make them both a fortune.

It never happened.

Then there was the idea of getting an artist to paint Hercules' face on the back of shirts, which, when sold in sufficient quantity, would make them both a fortune.

That never happened either.

Not to mention the time in the gambling hall when he invented something called the Happy Hour, a specific time of day when all drinks were sold at half price, to such an extent that it would, unquestionably, make him a fortune.

The profits were, to say the least, disappointing.

Just watching him think made Hercules tired.

Listening to him explain how this scheme or that invention would rake in the dinars and fat purses of gold was enough to exhaust him more than battling a small army or one of Hera's assassination-minded monsters.

"So how would you like to get rich?" Salmoneus finally asked.

Hercules stared at the broad backs of the horses. He said nothing. He indicated nothing. He did his best not to breathe.

A Salmoneus idea, no matter how ingenious or ridiculous, never ever went anywhere without its close cousin—utter disaster.

*Cousin*, in fact, was the wrong word.

Twin was more like it.

It wasn't Salmoneus' fault . . . most of the time; it just happened that way.

"This time," Salmoneus continued confidently, "it's going to work. I know it. I can feel it. I can almost taste it."

Hercules grunted.

"You want to know what it is?"

Hercules looked at him steadily. "No, Salmoneus, I don't."

Salmoneus smiled. A broad smile. A trademark smile that underlined his unbounded optimism. "Sure you do."

"I suppose you'll tell me whether I want to know or not."

Flovi broke into an operatic rendition of "The Last Time I Saw Athens." Some of the notes were damn close. Even the horses' ears stopped twitching for a few bars.

Without warning Salmoneus' expression slipped from good cheer to concerned. A bad sign; and if the wagon hadn't been rumbling across another bridge, Hercules would have considered jumping.

"Actually," the man admitted, "I kind of need your help."

"No."

Salmoneus' eyes widened in shock. "No?"

"Right."

"You said no?"

"Yep."

"But . . . but . . . but you can't say no!"

Hercules kept his gaze on the horses. "Yes, I can. No."

"But you're Hercules!"

"Yep."

"Hercules never says no to someone in trouble."

"Sure he does. He does it all the time. A couple of times a day, in fact. Trust me, I've heard him."

The wagon tilted over a large rock. When it thumped back to the ground, Hercules grabbed the side with one hand to keep from falling off, and braced himself for Salmoneus' next attempt.

Oddly, it didn't come.

For the next mile or so, save for Flovi's light-hearted search for the melody in "Aphrodite Is My Temple Baby," there was silence. It would have been a welcome silence had not Hercules felt so guilty. Which made him mad. Which made him angry that he was mad because he felt guilty. Which made him uncomfortable because he knew Salmoneus was right—he hardly ever turned anyone down who needed his help. And that made him even angrier.

And more guilty.

He cleared his throat, a grudging, *this had better be good* signal that he was willing to listen.

Still Salmoneus said nothing. He concentrated on his driving.

Flovi, meanwhile, had switched to what was apparently his own composition, something about Man's search for Truth in a world where the gods kept switching reality around when Man wasn't looking, which rather defeated the purpose of searching for the Truth.

Not to mention the right notes.

Hercules said, "I'll be back," jumped off the wagon, waited until Flovi drew up beside him, and said, "Do me a favor and keep quiet for a while."

Flovi puffed his cheeks in indignation, his long mustache fairly fluttering. "I'm an artist, sir. A composer. A musician. I don't do favors like that."

"I saved your life. Make an exception."

Flovi harrumphed, stroked his mustache, and finally, reluctantly, nodded. "But if the Muse comes," he yelled defiantly as Hercules trotted away, "I shall not turn her away!"

If the Muse comes, Hercules thought, she's dumber than I thought. And stone deaf, too.

Once back in his seat, he jabbed Salmoneus' shoulder none too gently and said, "Talk to me, friend." He smiled. "I'll regret it, I know, but talk to me."

Salmoneus looked at him with brown eyes so sad Hercules wanted to pop him. "Are you sure?"

Hercules' look told him not to push it.

Salmoneus took the point. "I was in Athens," he began.

It was intended to be a quick trip, primarily to collect an outstanding debt from a goldsmith of his acquaintance. No problems there; the man paid, they went to dinner, talked about old times, and eventually, through no fault of Salmoneus', ended up at the amphitheater.

That's where he discovered his destiny. His calling. His ticket to an earthbound Olympus, populated by himself and a zillion beautiful women instead of a bunch of cranky gods.

24

"Have you ever been?" he asked. "To one of those performances, I mean."

Hercules nodded. Carefully. Even the most innocuous of Salmoneus' questions often concealed traps.

"I couldn't believe it. All those seats filled, all those boys and girls running around with food to sell, all those men outside selling admission—I nearly passed out from the excitement."

"You're not . . ." Hercules couldn't bring himself to say it.

Salmoneus laughed. "Good heavens, no. I'm not going to build an amphitheater. What kind of a dope do you think I am?"

How much time do you have? Hercules thought, and pinched himself for it. Not, however, terribly hard.

Salmoneus lifted a dramatic finger. "These actors came out, all wearing the same clothes, each holding a mask in front of his face. It was a play." He made a face. "Something icky about frogs. But!" He shook the finger. "*But,* Hercules, the important thing was the people! I, being a democratic sort, sat in the cheap seats so I could observe my fellow man and take, as it were, the pulse of the populace." He glanced sideways. "And do you know what I learned?"

Hercules refused to answer.

The finger jabbed at the sky. "They were bored, Hercules! Bored out of their tiny Athenian skulls!"

"Considering the play was about frogs, I'm not surprised."

Salmoneus shook his head. That wasn't the point.

The point, he explained, was that outside the amphitheater were musicians and other street performers, and there, *there* the people were having a grand, wonderful, absolutely marvelous time.

"And," he added, lowering his voice, "they weren't from the city."

He waited.

Hercules waited.

"You don't see it."

"No."

Salmoneus scratched at his beard. "They wanted to be entertained."

"Okay."

"They had to get it in the street, not in the amphitheater."

"Okay."

"They had to come to Athens to get the entertainment in the street, not in the amphitheater."

Hercules held up a hand for a moment of silence while he tried to take a few leaps ahead, if only to shorten the story. When he landed, he said, "Ah."

Salmoneus made a fist. "Ah."

"Ah . . . what?"

"Ah . . ." Salmoneus lifted the finger again. "What if someone were to bring the entertainment to the people, instead of the people going to the entertainment?" He held up a second finger. "What if someone were to provide not only the entertainment, but the food?" He held up a third finger. "What if someone charged a modest fee for the food and the entertainment, and gave a portion of it to the com-

munity wherein the food and entertainment were . . .
uh . . . were.''

Hercules pinched himself again, this time because
the idea almost actually made sense, and it was beginning to frighten him. Not the idea itself; the fact
that it almost made sense.

"You go to a small town or large village,'' Salmoneus explained, practically bouncing on the seat.
"You provide what the Thracians call a 'vaudal,' an
evening's show, and do you know what you have?''

"A fortune?'' Hercules guessed.

"Vaudalville!'' Salmoneus announced grandly,
rising from his seat, arms and reins spread. "Get it?
*Vaudal,* meaning entertainment; *'vill,'* from village.'' He laughed. "Laughs! Tears! Thrills! Wonders! And all for the price of a few measly dinars!''

"Sit down,'' Hercules said.

Salmoneus sat.

"Vaudalville?'' Hercules looked for the disaster,
found the potential for several dozen without half
working at it, and said, "No.''

"No? Again? No what?''

"Principle,'' Hercules told him. "Just a matter of
principle.''

They rode on.

Flovi began clearing his throat, testing his vocal
cords for the notes buried there.

"Six months,'' Salmoneus said at last.

"Really?''

"Six months, and you're not going to believe it,
but it's working.''

Hercules waited until the temptation to say the

obvious had passed. Then, before he knew what he was doing, he said, "So why do you need my help?"

"Because I think somebody," Salmoneus answered, "is trying to ruin me." He shook his head at such a disgusting notion. "That's why I need you, Hercules. Strange things have been happening. Really strange things."

Out of an acute sense of impending doom, Hercules declared that he didn't want to hear it.

Salmoneus, whose only sense of doom was sparked by an empty purse or dinner table, told him anyway.

# 4

In the beginning, Virgil Cribus believed he had about the best job in the world. He traveled, he saw sights he had never dreamed he would see, he met all kinds of interesting people, and he alone was responsible for the arrangements that made the Salmoneus Traveling Theater of Fun such a great success.

Lately, however, he figured he was lucky he still had his scalp.

He supposed it was his face. He looked much younger than he really was, even with the splotchy beard he'd been trying to grow over the past couple of weeks. People just didn't feel much like beating up a kid. Which he wasn't. And until now, he had vehemently denied he was.

So far, he had been lucky.

He had arrived in the small town of Phyphe late last night. This morning, energized by decent sleep and a good meal, he had hit Phyphe like a hurricane. Fast talk, sincere smiles, a nudge and a wink, and

by midday he had secured rooms for the entire vaudalvillian troupe at a price Salmoneus would be
proud of.

The hardest part had been Dragar's place. The
man insisted on remaining apart from all the others.
"To practice, and to keep my secrets from being
stolen" was the reason. Luckily no one ever argued.
He was, Virgil had to admit, a damn weird man,
even for a magician, and the others were glad they
didn't have to share the same roof with him.

Having completed that task, Virgil ate a quick
lunch and strolled to the center of town.

From what he had learned so far, Phyphe had been
founded either by an astute group of businessmen
looking for a way to consolidate their shops along
one of the area's primary caravan and travel routes,
or by a bunch of drunks who stopped here because
they couldn't walk any farther.

Either way, it made for an interesting setup.

Phyphe was shaped like a wheel.

All the streets were spokes out of the center, the
main street being twice as wide as the others, leading
to the road that made its way through the surrounding hills and valleys.

Just outside town, in a field west of the road, was
Phyphe's somewhat petite version of a big-city coliseum: two crescents of six rows each, facing a small
paving-stone floor where the community's major
events were celebrated. Virgil estimated a hundred
people could fill this coliseum; two or three, if they
didn't take deep breaths. Between the crescents, gaps

barely the width of two men walking abreast provided entrance and exit.

The outer stone wall was the biggest problem. Despite its height, a quick survey of the surrounding area made him suspect a lot of folks just climbed to the roofs of the nearest buildings to watch whatever was going on. For free. Something would have to be done about that. Perhaps—

"Ah, Virgil, there you are," a husky voice said.

He prayed for strength, resolution, and, in a pinch, invisibility.

This was the most difficult part of all his assignments—negotiating with town leaders for percentages of the profits. Unfortunately Phyphe had a leader of the leaders, and last night it was clear she had more in mind than just a simple handshake to close the deal.

"Olivia," he said warmly, fixing a welcoming smile in place as he turned. He made a show of checking the sun. "Right on time. Wonderful. Wonderful."

Olivia Stellas was of indeterminate age. Her face was smooth and taut. Very taut. So taut that Virgil wondered when he first saw her why her ears were still on the sides of her head. Her hair was incredibly, unnaturally black and long, and elaborately braided into a high cone-like pile, with two coy curls dangling at her temples; there wasn't a doorway in town she could walk through without ducking. Her lips were thick and red, her eyes dark and unreadable, her nose the only feature that had sharp angles.

Virgil had a feeling that whenever she walked on

31

the beach, sharks for hundreds of miles around ducked for cover.

She linked her arm with his and led him into the arena, gliding, eyes shifting constantly, head up as if testing the air.

"My sources tell me you've had troubles recently."

"Rumors," he assured her, patting her hand and suppressing a shudder. "Jealous rivals."

"The earth tremors?"

"Coincidence."

"The fire?"

"A drunk knocked a torch over at the entrance."

"The riot?"

He grinned. "Three men fighting over Miss Delilah, our contortionist."

"Hyanth?"

They stopped in the center.

"Really, Olivia," he said. "A man turned into a frog?" He laughed as a man of the world laughs with a woman of the world at the way rumors persist in the lives of the rubes of the world.

Olivia didn't laugh. She smiled. Tautly.

Virgil shuddered again, especially when she bumped her hip against his and suggested they repair to the nearest quiet place in order to complete the arrangements.

He agreed.

She winked.

He thought, I want a raise.

• • •

In the beginning, Dragar only wanted to be a competent trickster—a man who could pull rabbits and rats out of a cap, pull ribbons out of his ear, and make people laugh when he pulled a dinar from the nose of an unsuspecting audience member.

As a young man he had been short and dumpy; as a young man he had a terrible stutter; as a young man he had been tormented and beaten up and shunned and reviled.

As a young man he had been a lousy magician. He had little flair, little skill, and every time he lowered his arms, a chicken fell out of his sleeve.

Dragar Illarius didn't want to be a magician anymore.

He wanted more.

Much more.

He stood in the center of the room that mop-head, Virgil, had secured for him, and scanned the chests that held his props. He was no longer short, no longer dumpy; he no longer stuttered, and no longer cared whether people liked him or not.

"You want the big bed or the little one?"

He closed his eyes briefly. "The big one, of course," he said to the woman in the adjoining room.

"You always get the big one."

"I'm the star. I deserve it."

Aulma came to the connecting door and put her hands on her hips. Nice hips, Dragar thought as an unbidden smile touched his lips; nice everything else, too, but really nice hips.

She pouted. A practiced pout he had seen a hundred times, and ninety-nine times it had almost worked. The one time it had worked she didn't have anything on but her long blond hair, so he didn't count it.

"I'm hungry," she said, still pouting while she fluffed her hair.

"I have work to do."

"You always have work to do."

He smiled, and smiled more widely when she took an involuntary step back. He had smiles and he had smiles, and this smile was the one that reminded her of her station, and what would happen if she tried to raise it. Or forget it.

She glanced at the far corner.

He didn't look; he didn't have to.

It was there. He could feel it. He could feel the energy that cloaked it like a veil. He could feel the promise it had made when he created it, six months ago.

He could feel the power.

"It's glowing," she whispered fearfully.

"It's all right," he assured her. "Nothing to fear." *As long as I'm around* was the unspoken warning.

She licked her lips nervously, her hands clasped to her chest. "I . . ." She swallowed. "When we got here last night?" She swallowed again. "I felt it, Dragar." A tentative smile. "I think I really felt it."

So had he.

As soon as he had stepped into the middle of this pathetic town's pitiful excuse for a crass coliseum, he had felt the tingle work its way up his spine, spread across his shoulders, and down to his fingers. So disgusted was he by the venue, he had been taken by surprise when the feeling struck him.

"Four," she said, daring a step into his room.

He nodded.

"The last?"

He nodded again, once, slowly.

Another step, close enough for her to take his hand. "And then what?"

He pulled her into an embrace, holding her head against his chest while he looked at the eyes that glowed and pulsed in the corner.

You have no idea, he thought grimly; my dear, you have no idea what I'm going to do now.


"I'm going to be a star!" Merta declared angrily. "Nothing you can do will stop me. I'm going to travel to every kingdom and make kings grovel at my feet. I'm going to make a fortune and have a kingdom of my own. I'm going to make Zeus so jealous, he'll make me a goddess in charge of all the gold and silver in the world! That's what I'm going to do and no one is going to stop me!"

She inhaled sharply, held the breath until her cheeks began to quiver, then exhaled in such a rush that she became light-headed and had to sit on the stool behind her.

Still, it was a good speech. A few more practices, and she'd actually give it to someone besides the jackass.

Which, in its stall, snorted, twitched its ears, and

grabbed another mouthful of hay. It didn't seem terribly impressed.

"Really," she told it. "As soon as they get here, I'm going to audition, they'll make me a star, and I'm gone. Outta here. No more mucking about." She glared around the eight-stall stable. "Absolutely no more mucking about."

The jackass chewed.

In the last stall to her left a bony gray mare hung its head over the door and flubbered its lips.

"Yeah, yeah," she said. "Easy for you to say."

The mare flubbered again.

Merta sighed, and began humming. She had a good voice. She knew she had a good voice. Everybody who heard her told her she had a good voice. The trouble was, the people who heard her were the same people who had heard her all her life, and they never paid for listening.

But ever since she had seen the notices announcing the imminent arrival of the Salmoneus Traveling Theater of Fun, she knew her destiny was on the way. This Theater thing had already garnered great attention, travelers passing word of marvels and wonders and thrills and laughs, and, most importantly, it was worth every dinar. Some had even seen it three and four times.

Destiny, she thought longingly; my destiny has arrived.

The mare flubbered.

The jackass kicked the wall.

Her mother yelled from the corral, something

about the pig getting its head caught in the fence again.

Merta burst into song as she got to her feet.

Destiny.

And the jackass's ears stopped twitching.


Just to the east of Phyphe the forest had been cleared for farmland. A wide stream flowed through it, making its way from the hills to the west, across the fields and into the trees again, where it meandered until the land abruptly dropped. The resultant waterfall was nearly fifty feet high, the frothing pool at its base deep and long and rich with life. The downstream water was deeper still, and fishermen loved it. Lovers did, too, sitting on the grassy banks beneath the shade of ancient oak and myrtle, sipping wine, eating bread, fooling around. Children played here. Old men and old women reminisced here.

A young stag stepped cautiously out of the trees near the pool. It sniffed the air, checked the rocky bank across the way, and remained motionless for several long seconds before dipping its head to drink.

It never saw the flash of sharp green fire.

# 5

The road to Phyphe split just on the other side of a fast-running clear stream. Hercules watched the two wagons until they rumbled out of sight, slipping around a bend choked with high brush. They had taken the right fork; he took the left, where the road eventually narrowed and followed the stream northward.

He wanted time to think. To consider. Maybe to figure out a way he could deny Salmoneus' request for help without hurting the man's feelings. He certainly couldn't do any of that while Salmoneus prattled and Flovi sang and the horses threatened to revolt.

The sound of the water was soothing; the serenity of the woodland was calming.

He walked slowly, now and then watching the sunlight flare off the stream's surface, now and then looking for a stout branch he could use to whack himself on the skull for even thinking about getting involved.

Still, he had to admit that Salmoneus' problem was intriguing.

He just wasn't sure where exaggeration ended and the truth began.

During the past half year, the genial hustler had decided to expand his vaudalville idea into something far more complex than a simple traveling sideshow. Permanent theaters or arenas in several towns were the goal, each spaced far enough apart so there would be little overlap in what he called the customer base. Acts would rotate among the theaters regularly: continuous entertainment, never the same performers twice in one month, low prices, guaranteed fun, and not a single play about frogs among them.

Salmoneus had slapped a thigh for emphasis. "When it's settled, my friend, all I'll have to do is sit back and count the dinars, weigh the gold."

"You won't manage them yourself?"

"Of course not. I can't be in all those places at the same time. I'm not a god, you know, like some people I know."

"Ah." Hercules finally spotted the flaw. At least, the first flaw he could pick out among all the others clamoring for his attention. "So you'll—"

"Handpick my managers. Absolutely. Trusted men and women who will—"

"Rob you blind," Hercules finished with a grin. "But if anything goes wrong, you get the blame."

Salmoneus started to protest, considered, tucked his tongue into the corner of his mouth and considered a while longer, shook his head, reformulated the protest, and finally slumped back in exhaustion.

"Not that it *will* happen," Hercules said quickly to the dismay on his friend's face. "You'll just have to be careful, that's all. As," he added as sincerely as he could without breaking into hives, "you always are."

"It's a good idea," Salmoneus muttered petulantly.

"Of course it is."

"A bountiful idea."

"No question about it."

"An entertainment innovation never before seen by the human race."

"Not even by the gods."

"You're lying to protect my feelings."

Hercules grinned again. "Through my teeth."

Salmoneus came within a hair's breadth of losing his temper, sagged again, and laughed, this time ruefully. "I do get enthusiastic, don't I."

Hercules nodded.

"But I know it'll work, Hercules. I *know* this will work. If only I could find out who didn't want it to."

Protection of the idea, however, was not why Hercules had agreed to think about endorsing Salmoneus' scheme. If only half the tales of woe his friend had told him were accurate, this venture had turned into something quite a bit more than one rival trying to sabotage another.

Especially since, in this case at least, Salmoneus had no rivals.

**40**

In one village a small flood had wiped out half the crops; Salmoneus claimed there hadn't been a cloud in the sky all day. The villagers kept their rites on schedule, so a cranky god wasn't the answer either. It had just . . . happened.

Another village had nearly burned down when an alleged pillar of fire appeared briefly outside the building where the performances were being held. That the pillar lasted only a few seconds was the main reason only a shop was leveled, and a couple of eyebrows singed.

Fights had broken out in otherwise peaceful audiences; Miss Delilah the Contortionist's costumes had been slashed to ribbons; the jugglers, Clova and Aeton, claimed they had been poisoned; unknown thieves had robbed three taverns in three different towns.

"And in Hyanth," Salmoneus concluded, nearly wailing, "some kid was turned into a yellow frog!"

Hercules didn't bother to hide his disbelief.

"Really, Hercules, I'm not kidding. Poof! Man one minute, frog the next." Salmoneus shrugged. "Most amazing thing I ever saw."

"A . . . frog."

"Well," he said grudgingly, "I'm sure it was a trick of some kind. Dragar—he's one of my main attractions—says only a god can turn a man into a frog."

"Who's Dragar?"

"A magician."

"Magician?"

"Magician. You know—dinars out of noses, rib-

**41**

bons from your ears, that sort of thing." Salmoneus shrugged. "Actually, he's really quite good. You'll like him. Well, not him, personally. Personally, he's a little bit on the dim side, and very forgetful. He's also kind of a snob. Thinks he's ready for the big time and keeps asking for more money." He laughed a little. "What he doesn't know is, he *is* in the big time. Or as big as it gets around here."

And so it had gone, one minor disaster after another. Word spread. Engagements had been canceled. Threats had been made. Money was lost. Salmoneus was being hurt where it hurt the most—right in the heart of his purse.

Hercules couldn't find the branch, but he did find a large pool that spread from the base of a beautiful, narrow waterfall. Since he couldn't decide what to do about Salmoneus, he decided to do something about the afternoon's heat. He stripped quickly, stretched, and dove in.

The water was clear, and he grinned at the small colorful fish who scooted away when he invaded their world. A push off the rocky bottom brought him back to the surface; a deep breath sent him under again, listening to the muted thunder of the waterfall, watching the seductive sway of underwater plants leaning in and out of the languid twisting current.

Only when his lungs began to burn did he head up, fast, breaking into the air explosively, gasping for breath, laughing aloud, and grateful that the cool water had cleared his head.

And suddenly aware that he wasn't alone.

He turned, and blinked in astonishment at the woman treading water behind him.

He blinked again when she yelled, "How dare you!" and slapped him a good one right in the jaw.

He went under, came up sputtering, and went down a second time when she slapped him again.

This time he took no chances. He stayed under and swam for shore, using submerged rocks as a makeshift staircase to bring him to the grassy bank. Once out, he fumbling hastily into his pants and reached for his boots.

He spotted the woman on the other side, ducking behind a large bush.

Although the waterfall was a good hundred feet away, its constant thunder thwarted his attempts to call out an apology. Instead, he finished dressing, using his sleeveless shirt to dry his chest and arms. Then he spread it on the grass beside him for the sun to do its work.

Much to his disappointment the woman remained hidden.

Not that he would soon forget her.

From the glimpse he had gotten before she'd slugged him, he knew she was lovely, that she had long blond hair darkened by the water, and that she had been absolutely naked.

He touched his jaw gingerly.

Her slap had been pretty good, too. He had a feeling she'd had lots of practice with that swing.

He smiled and shook his head. It figured. Salmoneus and a beautiful woman come into his life on the same day—one wanted him to save a business, the other wanted to take off his head.

He didn't bother looking around; he didn't think he'd be able to find a cave.

Yet it would be nice if, once dressed, she showed herself so he could tell her he was sorry. And seeing her again wouldn't be all that terrible either.

He tensed then, waiting for an all-too-familiar pang of guilt, and was a little surprised, and saddened, when it didn't happen. A long time had passed since the murder of his wife and children, and it had taken all of that time for him to finally understand that nothing he did was going to bring them back.

He missed them, and he knew that would never leave him. Nor would he ever be free of the ache that sometimes came in the middle of the night, when their absence was felt more strongly. When he was alone.

But they were gone.

Forever.

And he, whether he liked it or not, was still here.

He sighed, and wiped his face with a palm.

The woman remained out of sight.

A few minutes later, he decided she had left, had slipped into the trees and away. Ah well, he thought, and put on his shirt; another time, maybe.

He stood, massaged the back of his neck, and decided he might as well head for Phyphe and face Salmoneus. It was one thing to give assistance to those who needed it, those in danger or in need; it was something else again to see Salmoneus on his way to a fortune that, no matter how much the man protested, somehow didn't seem all that honest.

Besides, he was hungry.

One more glance at the opposite shore, and he headed for the road that would take him to the fork. He picked up a stone and tossed it at the stream, picked up another and skipped it across the surface.

When he reached for the third, however, he froze.

There on his right, by a large rock on the bank, was an uneven patch of black, as if the grass and the brush around it had been seared by fire.

Frowning, he poked at it, brought the residue on his fingers to his nose and sniffed.

Ash, and it was still warm.

Something else. Something about the smell that refused to identify itself.

Yet there was no sign a fire had been built here, nor was there any reason why one should have been. The ground sloped toward the stream; no one, experienced or not, would build a fire here. He hunkered down and balanced on his toes, searching for something that made sense.

Nothing did.

The brush and ground in the immediate area were untouched; there was no scent of smoke, no embers that he could see. But when he passed a palm over the center of the black patch, he could feel residual heat.

For an unnerving moment he thought Hera had tried to nail him with a lightning bolt while he'd been in the pool, but she had better aim than that.

Besides, she would have fried the pool in order to boil him; that was more her style.

It was curious, but it didn't seem threatening.

One more glance around, one more check of the opposite bank, and he braced himself on the ground with one hand, ready to stand and be on his way.

That was when he saw the bone under the bush.

Suddenly not wanting to touch the scorched area again, he found a long thin branch and used it to poke the bone into the open.

As soon as he saw what it was, a chill skittered along his spine.

It wasn't a bone at all; it was part of a stag's rack.

And there, by his right heel, was part of a hoof.

Now he recognized the smell—it was flesh.

Burned flesh.

# 6

The first thing Hercules noticed when he reached Phyphe was the small arena constructed just west of town.

The second thing he saw was the caravans pulled up alongside the arena, and the crowd of children milling around them excitedly.

The third thing was a blur of billowing gold and white speeding toward him. Before he could get out of the way, the blur embraced him hard enough to take the breath from his lungs and nearly knock him off his feet.

"Hercules! I knew you wouldn't fail me! I knew it, I knew it! You're a man of honor who deserves his own palace on Olympus!"

Hercules looked down at the partially bald skull and sighed with a pained smile. "Salmoneus, I think—"

But Salmoneus grabbed his arm and tugged him toward the wagons. "Come, come, you have to meet the others." He lowered his voice. "They don't know who you really are, though. And watch out for Dragar. I think he's practicing picking pockets or something.''

''Salmoneus, we have to talk.''

''Later, later, there's no time now. Don't you see what joy I've brought to this miserable little place? Can't you see the goodness of my work?''

Actually, Phyphe didn't seem to be all that miserable. The buildings Hercules could see appeared well constructed and clean, and the people did not appear to be suffering from abject, or even remote, poverty.

He stopped abruptly, nearly yanking Salmoneus off his feet. ''We have to talk,'' he insisted.

At which point a young blonde in an outfit guaranteed to make Aphrodite gnaw jealously on one of her golden apples walked up, said, ''You again!'' and slapped Hercules a good one before stomping away.

Salmoneus gaped. ''Wow,'' he said. ''That usually doesn't happen to me until after the first night.''

Hercules only grinned. He might have taken offense had he not noticed that she had been blushing when she struck him. Which, he figured, meant she had seen him as well. Very well, in fact.

''Aulma,'' Salmoneus said in quiet wonder. ''She's usually such a gentle girl.''

''You know her?''

''Sure. She's Dragar's assistant.'' He frowned. ''That's him over there.''

He pointed to a man of medium height standing in the midst of a swarm of children. His hair was black and cropped close to his skull; his goatee was trimmed to a dagger's point; his face, although young, was more angles than flesh. He wore a purple robe, with a low stiff collar edged in silver and billowing sleeves, and gleaming black boots, and his waist was girdled by a thick silver rope. While his left hand held a shepherd's crook, his right busily burrowed in the hair of a little girl who couldn't stop giggling.

Dragar smiled, widened his eyes in mock surprise, and pulled a long yellow scarf from behind the child's ear. The other children, all of whom had colorful scarves of their own, applauded and laughed, and raced away in gleeful hysterics when he shooed them with the crook.

Then he spotted Salmoneus and hurried over, nearly tripping on the robe and clipping himself on the chin with the crook. "Salmoneus, I must speak with you, sir."

A sonorous voice that did not quite match the man's stature.

He was also much older than Hercules had first imagined. Fine lines sketched webs around his eyes and mouth, and a handful of silver-gray strands in his hair at the temples betrayed his true age.

"Later, later, Dragar," Salmoneus told him. "Much to do, so little time. You know how it is. I'll see you at dinner." He fluttered his fingers at both of them and escaped into a crowd of curious onlookers.

"Well," Dragar huffed. He gave Hercules what was either a smile or a vivid indication of a terrible attack of gas. "And you must be the new act. Wonderful, wonderful." He frowned. "I guess. What is it that you do?"

Hercules had no idea, and no idea how to bluff his way out of it.

"Ah, yes." The crook stamped the ground. "Ah!" Dragar hissed and stepped back, shaking the foot the crook had jabbed. "Clumsy of me, so sorry." He held out a hand, Hercules shook it, and the magician winced. "The strongman. I was right."

"Yes," Hercules answered quickly. "Salmoneus thought it might be fun."

"Of course he would. He's an idiot. No offense, of course."

"None taken." Hercules nodded toward the children, now gathered around the wagons. "That was nice, what you did for them."

Dragar closed one eye before he nodded. "Oh, yes, the scarf thing. Easier than the chicken thing, let me tell you. I don't sneeze as much anymore, either." His laugh was a series of rapid snorts. "Nice to meet you, sir. Practice. I must go off and practice. I suggest you do the same. Can't be too careful these days, you know. Talent comes and goes like the wind. Here today, gone tomorrow, you're stuck in an alley, begging for chickens." He coughed. "I mean, dinars."

A grand sweep of his hand in what was meant to be a courtly bow ended up with a large white duck falling out of his sleeve.

Hercules was too astonished to laugh.

The duck began to waddle away, turned abruptly,

and aimed some vicious pecks at Dragar's toes.

"Oh," the magician said, poking at the bird with the crook. "Oh. Dear me. My, don't do—" He poked again and danced out of the way. "Mercy, that hurts. I say, don't do that."

The bird finally gave up and waddled off, quacking to itself, clearly in a foul mood and aiming its beak at anyone who came near.

Dragar blinked rapidly, seemed ready to speak, then nodded a farewell and wandered away, oblivious to the commotion around him, his crook sweeping ahead of him to clear a path. By the time he was out of sight, Hercules had decided that simply whacking Salmoneus would be too easy. For getting him into this madness, a long vacation in the middle of a thorn bush would be much more satisfying.

Still, as he headed for the arena, he knew he shouldn't be surprised at anything his friend did. Or didn't do. Or, more to the point, didn't say. What he had to do from now on was try to keep a step ahead of the man and hope he wasn't trod on the heels and tripped.

A futile wish, perhaps, but one he made anyway. Just in case someone in charge of his destiny was paying attention.

Getting to the arena apparently wasn't part of it, though. He was waylaid by Flovi and a young man named Virgil, and spent the rest of the afternoon carting crates and trunks to the various inns where the troupe had its rooms. He didn't mind. It gave him a chance to see the rest of Phyphe, and to note that his initial impressions were correct: it was a pleasant, fairly prosperous community that, because of its isolation, was close to giddy about the excitement Salmoneus had brought it.

He didn't see Dragar again, or his lovely assistant.

He did meet Clova and Aeton Junarus, however, the juggling and tumbling act. Salmoneus had told him they were brother and sister, twins from the mountains to the north. Which, he thought, might explain their attitude. What it didn't explain was their fine clothes and Clova's glittering jewelry. Whatever Salmoneus paid, Hercules knew it couldn't be much.

"So," Clova said, eyeing him as if he were a cow to be judged for slaughtering, "you're the strong one." She wore her brown hair in a thick braid draped over her left shoulder. "You don't look it."

"Now, Clova," Aeton said chidingly. He smiled apologetically as one hand swiped long bangs from his eyes. "You'll have to forgive my little sister. She's not used to working with amateurs, I'm sure you understand."

They stood in front of the inn where Hercules' room had been booked. It was by far the smallest of those he had seen in town thus far; it was also the least elegant—by several long miles and a couple of obviously unused brooms.

"Amateurs," Hercules repeated flatly.

"Not to worry," the young man said cheerily. "You'll get the hang of it."

"Just stay out of our way," his sister said.

"Now, Clova."

Wisdom kept Hercules' mouth shut.

52

Clova eyed him again and shook her head slowly. "I don't see it, Brother. Salmoneus must have been feeling charitable, don't you think?"

"Now, Clova."

Wisdom, Hercules decided, wasn't all it was cracked up to be.

She patted his cheek in such a condescending way that he almost grabbed her braceleted wrist and flung her into the nearest wall. Instead, he held onto his rigidly polite smile and listened while Aeton explained that there was, as in all things, a certain pecking order among the stars of the vaudalville circuit. He, Hercules, being the newest member must perforce begin at the bottom and work his way up. He understood that, didn't he? Of course he did. Just be a good boy and nothing will go wrong.

Perforce? Hercules thought; the twerp really said perforce?

"Can we go now?" Clova whined. She glanced around and shuddered. "This place is so unsavory. It's making me sick to my stomach. Our God Leaf Inn is so much better, so much more . . ." She wrinkled her nose in concentration. "Civilized."

"Yes, Sister, right away." He slapped Hercules' arm in farewell and tilted his head in mild surprise. "My. You *are* a strong one, aren't you."

"As strong as I need to be," Hercules replied before he could stop himself.

Clova rolled her eyes. "Oh, really, how . . . how . . ."

"Uncouth?" Aeton suggested.

"Disgusting," Clova said.

"Now, Clova."

They walked away as quickly as they could without actually running, and Hercules had to force the tension from his neck and arms before he could go inside. Otherwise, he probably would have brought the roof down, and a couple of the walls as well.

Once inside, he was able to relax. The inn may have been on the far side of luxurious, but it was reasonably clean, and the food the barmaid served him with a giggle and a wink was more than passable. When he finished, he sat back, stretched out his legs, and ordered a rare, for him, goblet of mead.

Salmoneus joined him shortly afterward.

"Well? What do you think?"

"I think you're nuts," Hercules told him. "You're traveling with a bunch of loons."

Salmoneus waved and shrugged. "Of course they're loons. They're in show business." He folded his arms on the table and lowered his voice. "Have you found out anything yet? Do you know who's trying to ruin me?"

Hercules stared at him over the top of his goblet. "Salmoneus, I've just gotten here. I've spent most of the day helping Flovi unpack and take care of the wagons and horses. Besides, what am I supposed to be looking for?"

Salmoneus glanced side to side. "Whatever it was, Hercules, that changed your mind about helping me."

Hercules said nothing.

"That *is* what you wanted to talk to me about, isn't it?"

Hercules said nothing.

Salmoneus reached out and stabbed a finger against Hercules' arm, grimaced, and shook it gingerly. "Well? What's the matter?"

"You."

"Me?"

"You."

"What about me?"

"You."

Salmoneus tried several times to say something, tried several times more to figure out exactly what it was he wanted to say, and gave up by ordering a tankard of wine, half of which he drank without coming up for air.

"Okay. One more time—what about me?"

Hercules decided it would be cruel not to answer. "You. Just when I think I've got you all figured out, you surprise me."

Salmoneus wasn't sure that was a compliment, but he decided to take it as one by blushing a little, and drinking a lot more.

"I sometimes think," Hercules continued, "that you pay attention only to those things that concern you. Nothing else matters. You ask me to help out, I tell you I'll think about it, you automatically assume that I'm going to say yes. At least, that's what I assumed."

"Hercules, I'm hurt. I'm really hurt you would think that of me."

Hercules gave him the *gimme a break* look.

Salmoneus countered with the *what do you expect, it's me* look.

Hercules would have reacted with the *you could be straight with me for a change* look, but it was too complicated, too late in the day, and he was too tired to figure it out.

He was honest with his friend. He admitted his reluctance was born of a desire never again to get involved in one of his schemes. Then he told him about finding the remains of the stag.

For a few seconds Salmoneus and his wine didn't get it. When they did, he paled. "The pillar of fire?"

"I don't know."

"Well, it wasn't the flood."

"I don't know what it was, Salmoneus. Whatever happened, though, wasn't natural. And I can't help thinking that it's no coincidence you're here at the same time."

Salmoneus lowered his head until he could thump his brow against the table. "I knew it. I'm cursed." He looked up without taking his head off the table. "Is it the gods? Have I done something? This time, I mean. Have you heard anything? Do you know—"

"No," Hercules assured him. "I don't know anything, I haven't heard anything, and I doubt you've offended any of the gods more than you usually do." He grinned to take away the sting.

Salmoneus sat up and sighed. He stared stupidly at his wine, emptied the tankard, and hiccupped behind a hand. "I am going to bed," he announced carefully. "Alone. As always." He stood. "Good night, Hercules. I thank you for ruining my day."

"My pleasure."

Salmoneus laughed shortly and made his way to the door, stumbling into a pair of men just on their way in. They pushed and shoved a little before Salmoneus left, and the pair sneered at his back.

Hercules didn't move.

Sitting in a shadowy corner gave him an advantage he didn't want to lose. As long as they couldn't see him, he would take the time to wonder if this was yet another coincidence—that two of the men who had attacked Salmoneus' wagons that morning were now in Phyphe, these being the one with the curly hair and the one who was far more handsome than the others.

He doubted it was a coincidence.

Which meant he would have to stick around, and follow them when they left. Maybe they would lead him to the others.

They whispered to the bartender, something passed between them, and they settled at a table near the door without looking in his direction.

A few minutes later the bartender offered Hercules a free drink, seeing as how he was in show business and all, and probably famous. Although it was more than he usually drank, Hercules accepted graciously, sipping it once in a while so as not to cause offense.

An hour later, just when he was about to give up, the curly-headed thief laughed and pulled the handsome one to his feet. They left with their arms around each other's shoulders, and he gave them a few seconds before he stood up to follow.

That was as far as he got.

The room began to sway, his legs refused to work, and when he tried to sit down, he couldn't find the chair. He sat anyway, on the floor; he decided that was too much work and lay down, on the floor; he decided his eyes needed a rest, and he closed them.

The last thing he heard was a rough voice laughing softly.

# 7

Voices—he heard voices. Dimly. Distantly. As if he were eavesdropping from the darkest corner of the Underworld.

"I think he's dead."

"He's not dead, he's asleep."

"Looks dead to me."

"He's breathing. That means he's not dead."

"If he is who you say he is, how do you know that breathing means he's alive? Demigods aren't like you and me, you know. For one thing, they're demigods."

"Just hit him with the water, all right?"

"I don't know, Salmoneus. Hit a demigod with water, he might get ticked, and I don't want to tick off a demigod. He might take away my voice or something."

"Flovi, he's not going to take your voice. Believe me."

"Besides, he saved my life. I don't want him to get mad after he saved my life."

"Flovi, give me the jug."

"Not if you're going to hit him with the water I won't."

He felt a not so distant pounding somewhere in the recesses of his skull. It reminded him of a much earlier time, when he had been feeling so sorry for himself, so tired of living without his wife and children, that he had drunk what seemed like half a barrel of wine. The next morning he wasn't dead, but he certainly felt like it.

He knew he wasn't dead now, either.

But he certainly felt like it.

He also felt a gentle pat on his cheek.

"Hercules, wake up."

"Flovi, use your head for a change. That won't do it. Use the water."

"I am not using the water. Look at him. He's bigger than life, for crying out loud. Somebody bigger than life is not going to be happy if you hit him with water. Come on, Hercules, wake up, sir."

"Sir?"

"Well, what do you call him?"

"Hercules. That's his name."

"I can't believe you're a friend of his. You. Of all people."

"What's that supposed to mean?"

"Hercules. Sir. Wake up."

**60**

"By the gods, Flovi, if you don't hit him with the water, I'm going to hit him with you!"

Hercules opened his eyes just wide enough to make out two sightly blurred figures standing beside him. Looking down. Concerned. As if he were on the brink of dying. Which he knew he wasn't, even though he definitely felt like it. The pounding increased, there was a foul taste in his mouth, and although he hadn't stirred, he suspected that his arms and legs weren't going to work all that well.

"He's not moving, Salmoneus."
    "I can see that. Use the water."
    "Why don't *you* use the water?"
    "Are you nuts?"
    "All right, all right. Just make sure you tell him it was your idea. I don't want to lose my voice."

Hercules heard a low growling, a faint whimper, and saw one of the figures lift something off the floor.
    "I think," he said, "that's not a good idea."
    The two figures jumped, something crashed onto the floor, and for the next few moments there was a lot of jumping about, relatively mild cursing, and a lot of complaints about soaked sandals and shrinkage.
    Hercules raised himself cautiously on his elbows, gasped, closed his eyes, and fell back to wait for the world to stop spinning.
    He was in his room, that much he could tell. Why he was here, though, he didn't know. The last thing

61

he remembered was sitting in the inn, watching the two caravan thieves and wondering why they had happened to show up in Phyphe, of all places. Surely they understood that their victims would be able to recognize them. Were they that stupid?

"He's dead again."

Hercules groaned. "I am not dead." His eyes opened slightly; the world was still. A good sign. Maybe. "What happened?"

Salmoneus knelt beside the bed. "I don't know, Hercules. The innkeeper sent for me last night. He said you were dead, or passed out, and he wanted me to throw you into the street."

"Water," Hercules said weakly.

Salmoneus grinned at Flovi. "See? I told you."

"A drink," Hercules added quickly. "Lots of drinks. Of water."

"On my way," Flovi said eagerly. "Don't die before I get back."

For a moment there was silence.

Blessed silence.

Then: "Hercules, it's starting already."

Hercules rubbed a hard hand over his face, trying to force some life into it. "What is?"

"The disasters."

"I hardly think this counts as a disaster, Salmoneus."

"But the innkeeper's been talking to other innkeepers and tavern owners, and *they've* heard about the other places. They think your practically dying is part of . . . whatever. How did they know?"

"I'm not dying, Salmoneus."

"Well, I know that, but they don't. How did they find out?" Salmoneus frowned. "What happened? You drink too much?" His frown deepened, and a hand waved away an answer. "Never mind. You don't drink hardly at all. What did you have?"

"Mead." He held out a hand. "Help me up."

Between the two of them, they managed to get him upright and his legs over the edge of the bed. The world didn't spin, but his stomach did.

"One portion of mead?" Salmoneus moved back to the room's only chair, dropped into it, and shook his head. "I've heard of people having low tolerance for drink before, but . . ." He scratched at his temple. He scratched at his stomach. He glanced at the door, snapped his fingers, and said, "Powders."

"Potions," Hercules said at the same time.

They grinned at each other until the implication struck them like one of Aulma's slaps.

Salmoneus could do nothing better than shrug ignorance.

Hercules, his head still not quite sure it was going to stay hitched to his shoulders, didn't even try to come up with a solution. Someone who knew who he was, or someone who felt threatened, had drugged him. No attempted murder here; just getting him out of the way for the night.

"Anything happen?" he asked as Flovi returned with a new jug and a goblet. Hercules ignored the goblet, upending the jug instead, drinking some of the cool water, letting the rest trickle over his head.

"No," Salmoneus said. "At least not that I know of."

Flovi lifted his shoulders when they looked at him. "Nothing. Everybody was fine. No robberies, nobody around the wagons. I walked around the arena once to get the size of it, and went to my room to practice."

A puzzle, Hercules thought, his already foul mood souring even further. He hated puzzles. Thieves, warriors, armies, Hera, bullies—no puzzles there. Puzzles always meant there was more to what he saw than what he was looking at. It was the kind of thing that made a decent man dizzy, just trying to keep track of it all.

"You need food," Salmoneus decided, getting to his feet.

Hercules' stomach disagreed.

"Food, and hard work. That'll clear your brain."

Flovi hummed a few bars of something or other.

"Forget it," Salmoneus told him as they headed for the door. "Try me again when you can get through a whole song."

"I can," Flovi insisted.

"Not in one piece, you can't."

Hercules followed, saying nothing until he was faced with the innkeeper, who gave him a surprisingly long list of available foods. Just as surprisingly, he discovered he was starving and essentially told the man to begin at the beginning and not stop until he was told to.

Within an hour Hercules finally felt alive, if not perfect, and he spent the rest of the day helping the troupe set up.

The program was simple: a performance early the

following evening to whet the townspeople's appetite, no performance the next day, so that word could spread to the nearby villages and farms, then two straight evenings of entertainment before Salmoneus moved on.

It was more work than Hercules had imagined. Chests and trunks had to be brought to the right people; the wagons had to be stored and cleaned and, in one case, repaired; and he himself had become the object of much attention once it was learned he was not only a worker, he was part of the show.

The strongman.

Hercules hadn't been clear exactly what he was supposed to be until he heard Virgil Cribus making a street announcement—that any man who thought himself man enough could challenge the awesome Salmoneus Red Power Beast to a wrestling match. The prize: a purse of dinars.

Hercules followed him for nearly an hour, and in no instance was his true name revealed.

I knew it, he thought, not sure if he should be angry. Leave it to him to find a way to make a dinar off me, even when he's in trouble.

It was, almost, admirable.

On the other hand . . . Red Power Beast?

By sunset he was exhausted, and he still hadn't had an opportunity to get inside the arena. Every time he made an attempt, someone called him to help with a move or a construction or herding the kids out of the way.

It was also tiring trying to watch everyone he saw, looking for the malicious expression or the suspicious glance. Someone had drugged him. The reason why was still a mystery.

Flovi, evidently, had a mystery, too.

They sat on the lip of a large stone well just east of the arena, well away from the nearest building.

"This place," Flovi said, wiping his sweating face with an already damp cloth. "I don't know, but there's something about it."

The sun was below the treetops. Shadows had taken over the open space around the arena, and most of the children and adults gone to dinner.

Flovi cleared his throat and sang a few bars of "Moonlight on the Aegean."

Hercules only winced twice.

"Don't you feel it?" The man waved his left arm, his right held loosely against his wounded side. "My destiny is here, Hercules. I really think so."

"If you say so."

"I say so." Flovi slipped off the well and held both arms up to the star-filled sky. "Ouch."

"Go to bed," Hercules told him amiably. "You'll heal faster."

"My destiny," Flovi sang as he wandered off into the shadows.

Nuts, Hercules decided with a quick silent laugh; these people are all nuts. But at least Aulma hadn't slugged him again, and he decided he would make an effort to talk to her the next day. Apologize, if she would let him. Otherwise, he'd probably end up losing half his teeth.

One last note out of the darkness, amazingly clear

and smooth, and the moon took over the sky, the land below was cloaked in silver.

Hercules stretched, yawned, and admitted that he felt pretty good. The work hadn't been all that hard, the company—especially the children—had been fine, and other than the potion in the mead, he hadn't noticed anything out of the ordinary. The news of previous trouble was easy to explain: either a traveler had come through, or someone had spread the rumor from within the troupe. Finding that one wouldn't be all that difficult. Just ask a few questions.

End of trouble.

Right, he thought; and tomorrow you'll wake up with a ton of gold on your chest.

Another stretch, another yawn, and he turned to haul up the well's bucket for a last drink before heading off to his bed. As he turned the crank, however, he heard a curious sound.

He turned his head slowly.

Flickering lights there in town; moonlight awash across the grass and dirt; the low black hulk of the arena.

No one out there.

He heard it again.

He looked toward the seemingly solid wall of trees some thirty feet beyond the well, but he could not see or sense any movement there either.

A rustling, slow and steady.

Flexing his fingers to keep them loose, he side-stepped away from the well, braced himself as he cocked his head.

It was familiar, that sound.

He knew . . . He grinned.

Wings.

He looked up expectantly. "Hermes?"

Something large and heavy slammed into his back, knocking the air from his lungs as he landed hard on his chest.

"Think again, big boy," a harsh voice snarled. "You ready to die?"

# 8

The obvious response to the immediate situation would be to buck the attacker off, leap to his feet, and find out what in the name of Poseidon's tides was going on.

The other obvious, and more prudent, response was to lie there, cheek to the ground, and figure out what, exactly, the attacker had that ever so carefully threatened to puncture a number of holes in his sides and spine.

"Don't move," the attacker whispered in his ear. "Move, and you'll be sorry."

He opened his mouth.

"Don't!" the attacker warned. "Call for help, you're a sieve."

"Believe me, I wasn't going to." He kept his voice quiet and even, to prevent whoever it was from panicking. Which, considering the circumstances, the attacker probably wasn't very likely to do. "What do you want?"

A rasping chuckle, a shift of weight, and suddenly he had an idea.

"Don't hurt him."

Hercules turned his head as slowly as he could. Someone stood in the shadow of the trees. By the sound of the voice, it was a woman.

"Won't."

"Promise?"

"Of course I don't promise. He tries to get away, I'll have to . . . you know."

Hercules felt rather than saw the shadow shudder.

"All right," she said reluctantly. "Just be careful, please?"

Something landed in front of his nose. He stared at it so hard he nearly went cross-eyed.

It was a feather.

I'll be, he thought.

The shadow left the trees, and he shifted his attention to the moon-drenched woman who walked cautiously toward him. Her long hair was dark and parted in the center, held off her face by a wide dark band—a gently rounded face, despite the night, clearly young, but not so young that he couldn't appreciate the beauty there.

She held out a hand. "Do you have to do that?"

"What do you think?" the rasping voice snapped. "He's a man. He'll cut us as soon as look at us."

It was enough.

"You know," he said, "it's been a long time, Agatra, but I don't think I've changed all that much."

He tensed as talons gripped more tightly, and a

70

face appeared over his left shoulder. He almost went cross-eyed again, but he managed to smile. "Hi."

"You!"

"Who?" the woman asked nervously.

"Him," Agatra snarled, clearly disappointed she wasn't going to get to skewer anyone tonight. She did not, however, lift herself off his back. She climbed off, leaving, he was sure, several deliberate punctures along his sides. "Nuts."

Hercules waited a second before pushing himself to his hands and knees, then rocked back onto his heels and grinned at the Harpy squatting in front of him. "You look pretty good."

She glared at him. "I should slit your throat and eat your innards."

"Agatra!" the young woman protested.

"She has a short memory," Hercules told the woman without taking his gaze from the Harpy. "I saved her life once, and she hates it."

Agatra lowered her head and spread her impressive wings. "Don't push it," she warned.

Hercules just grinned.

Some years before, in stark mountains that gave birth to winds that snarled with cold no matter what time of year, Hercules had come across a Harpy nesting area hidden deep in a cheerless valley.

Ordinarily he would have moved on immediately. Harpies were not the most even-tempered or hospitable creatures in the world on the best of days, and he had, on more than one occasion, battled more than a few to save the lives of humans.

This time, however, he could not leave.

The valley was under siege by a number of satyrs, who seemed bent on complete extermination of the community.

The Harpies were outnumbered, many of them already gravely wounded, and it was clear that the satyrs were on the brink of achieving their goal.

He didn't know why, but he had waded into the battle without a second thought.

The satyrs who survived fled.

Except one, who had a badly wounded Harpy trapped in a niche between two huge boulders. The creature had little intention of making an easy kill. First it wanted torment and torture.

Hercules lost his temper.

The satyr lost its life.

"Who are you?" the Harpy had demanded weakly, bleeding from a score of wounds, one broken wing hanging grotesquely from her shoulder.

"Hercules."

"I'm Agatra," she had said, gasping. "I'll remember you. Now leave, before the others kill you."

He had, and until now, had not seen Agatra again.

The young woman introduced herself and glanced apprehensively at the village. "Maybe we should . . ." She nodded toward the trees. "You know."

Agatra didn't move except to settle the feathers on her chest. "I'm not afraid."

Peyra sighed. "It has nothing to do with being afraid, Agatra. It has to do with our plan."

"What plan?" Hercules wanted to know.

"None of your business," the Harpy snarled.

"Agatra, come on," Peyra chided. "Maybe he can help us."

"He's a man."

"Well . . ." Peyra scanned Hercules boldly head to foot. "Yes, that's for sure."

"What plan?"

"Keep your mind on business," Agatra scolded.

"I am."

"Not that business, the other business."

Peyra, even in moonlight, clearly blushed.

Hercules, uncomfortable at the almost predatory look in her eyes and the way Agatra worked on her talons with a short piece of thin metal, suggested that they do as Peyra had suggested and get into the trees before they were spotted. He had no idea what they were up to, but he couldn't help feeling there was trouble involved.

There was always trouble involved.

The way things were going these days, he could smile at a squirrel and end up fighting a war.

Peyra insisted, and finally the Harpy trundled off, grumbling to herself about men, the long flight, and more men.

"I'm sorry," Peyra said as she and Hercules followed. "She's a little cranky."

"I know. I've seen."

"But we really could use your help, Hercules. Really."

Hercules shrugged. "I'd be glad to, of course, but I don't know what your trouble is."

"Frog," Agatra muttered. She had found a

twisted oak at the edge of the woods and was perched on its thick lower branch, not three feet above Hercules' head.

"Frog?"

"Frog," Peyra confirmed, and patted her stomach. Hercules stared.

Peyra gasped.

Agatra said, "Don't be silly, man. We're trying to get her husband back."

Hercules blinked. "Her husband?"

"The frog."

Hercules took a step back. "Her husband's a frog?"

"Well, he wasn't always a frog," said Peyra, insulted. "Why? Do I look like a frog, too?"

She's going to slap me, Hercules thought resignedly; there's a club, and now it's her turn to slap me.

"Oh, for crying out loud," Agatra snapped. "Will you two stop talking in circles? You're making me dizzy." She huffed to the ground and settled in front of Hercules. "Now, pay attention, man: This child and her husband were in Hyanth. They attended a performance of a traveling show. During the performance, a magician turned the husband into a frog." She nodded sharply. "Show him the frog, dear."

Quickly Hercules put up a hand. "Don't bother. I know what a frog looks like."

"It's yellow," the Harpy said in disgust. "A really ugly yellow."

Peyra sniffed back tears. "I don't want any trouble, Hercules. All I want is my Garus back."

Hercules looked at the darkened town. "And you think you'll get him back here?"

Her nod was tentative.

Hercules suggested quite sternly to himself that asking the question he was about to ask would only add to the problems he already had with Salmoneus. Add to them, complicate them, and, as usual, make his life miserable.

Peyra moved toward him and placed a soft hand on his chest. "Will you help me?"

Agatra groaned.

Hercules looked down into her eyes.

"Please?"

You know, he told himself when he discovered that a good part of him wasn't paying any attention, this really isn't—

She parted her lips ever so slightly.

Oh boy, he thought.

"The magician," he said hoarsely, and cleared his throat. "Do you remember the magician's name?"

Of course she does, you idiot, that inner voice sneered.

"Dragar," she answered breathily.

He would have laughed if it had not been for the plea in her expression, and the single tear that glowed in the corner of her left eye.

"I don't think so," he said gently.

"It was."

He put his hands on her arms, and instantly snatched them away when she leaned closer. "Peyra, listen, the kind of magic you're talking about is powerful stuff. It's the kind of magic reserved for the gods."

"I know," she said sorrowfully, but not so sorrowfully that she didn't rest her head against his chest and slip her arms around his waist.

"I've met this Dragar. He has good tricks, but I don't think he's smart enough to do what you say he did."

"But I saw it," she whispered, and tightened her arms.

Hercules couldn't help it—his arms embraced her.

"Careful," Agatra said disgustedly. "You'll squish the frog." And she added, "The one what's your husband, in case you've forgotten."

Peyra immediately jumped back, flustered, embarrassed, fussing with her hair.

Hercules reached out and grabbed her hands to keep them still. He smiled. "Look, I think you've somehow made a mistake. Dragar is, from what I've seen, very, very good at what he does. But he does tricks, not real magic. Don't you think it's possible you've been fooled?"

Peyra didn't hesitate: "No." She reached into the pouch at her waist and pulled out a yellow frog, which immediately rolled onto its back and stuck its legs out stiffly. "This is my husband." She sobbed as she slipped the amphibian back into its hiding place. "All I want is for Dragar to change him back. That's all. Nothing more."

Hercules looked to Agatra and asked *Do you believe this story?* without saying a word.

The Harpy nodded curtly.

Still, he wasn't sure. The power they attributed to Dragar was highly improbable. Even Hera wouldn't bestow such magic on a mortal, not even on her worst day.

But he had long ago learned that improbable did not mean impossible.

At that moment he recalled the list of disasters Salmoneus had recited. The drunken fights didn't concern him; the flood and the pillar of fire did.

If they were true, this went far beyond changing a kid into a frog. A really ugly frog.

With one hand to his mouth, he stared across the open field to the dark bulk of the arena, and the buildings beyond it.

"I can't promise anything," he said at last.

Peyra nearly sagged to her knees in relief.

Agatra snorted.

"You'll need a place to stay," Hercules said. "Trouble is, the town's full."

"Already have one," Agatra answered. She explained that they had found quite a comfortable cave near the waterfall. When he objected, more out of politeness than anything else, she reminded him that she wasn't exactly the usual tourist and would no doubt cause unnecessary trouble.

Peyra would stay with her.

Her tone brooked no argument, and since Peyra offered no opinion of her own, he had no choice but to accept the arrangement.

"The first performance is tomorrow afternoon, late. I'll meet you at the pool after sunset, let you know what I've learned."

Agatra grunted her acceptance and vanished into the shadows.

Peyra hesitated, then hurried up to him, kissed him soundly on the lips, and vanished as well into the darkness.

Hercules didn't move.

Although he often made light of Salmoneus' penchant for finding trouble without half trying, this was markedly, and ominously, different.

Signs and portents, he thought.

A breeze touched his face, and he turned away from it with a shudder.

It was too much like being touched by death.

# 9

Hercules stood outside the entrance to the Phyphe arena, his right hand absently rubbing his left arm as he felt an inexplicable reluctance to proceed any farther.

The clear morning sky had grown overcast, softening shadows and giving the intermittent breeze an unseasonable chill. A flock of birds flew over the town, their cries distant and melancholy. Somewhere behind him a horse whickered softly.

It was one of those odd moments in time, when everyone suddenly found other things to do, and he was alone, trying to shake off the uncomfortable sense that the town was deserted.

The arena's outside walls were smooth and windworn, at least twice again as tall as he was. He could see straight down the twenty-foot tunnel to the arena floor, and across to another entrance directly opposite.

All perfectly normal, all absolutely empty.

He felt foolish, and glanced over each shoulder,

sure that someone was watching, that he was the target of some bizarre trick.

Ordinarily he would have laughed it off and strode right in; ordinarily he would have figured that somehow Salmoneus was to blame.

He didn't.

Last night he had awakened an hour or so before dawn, not from a dream, but from the certainty that something had happened. His skin had been pocked with gooseflesh, and he could hear the restless stirring of animals in a nearby stable.

His first thought had been that the earth had moved. Not a quake, but a brief, slight shudder. He would have passed it off as the remnant of a dream had he not heard, in the dark, a distinct scrabbling sound. He used a flint carefully to light the candle by his bed, looked around, and saw tiny pieces of dirt and stone slipping off the windowsill to the floor.

The earth *had* moved.

And outside the window was a flicker of pale green.

He hadn't slept the remainder of the night, and no one he had spoken to this morning had admitted to experiencing the same thing.

He knew some of them had, though; he had seen it in their eyes, the way they refused to meet his gaze. He had seen it in the way a scavenging, black-and-white dog had shied away when he'd offered it scraps from his breakfast, as if he were going to beat it, not feed it.

Chiding himself, then, for letting his imagination

run free, he took a step into the tunnel, which had been roofed over with heavy thatch that allowed in little light. He grinned when nothing happened; took another step, and another, and hurried on, nearly laughing aloud.

Nice, he thought, a little relieved to reach the open arena. The smooth cobbled floor was shaped in an oval, perhaps seventy-five feet across its widest part. The interior wall rose just above his head, the rows ranged concentrically above, here and there decorated with fluttering ribbons. A small army of children had been through earlier, sweeping the stone flooring and seats, and hanging from the walls gold-and-blue bunting that rippled whenever the breeze coasted through the tunnels or over the top.

He checked the sky and sensed no approaching storm. There would be no sun for the performance, but no rain either.

Yet there was something . . . curious . . . about the place.

He frowned and took a step toward the center, stopping when a faint tingling rose from the soles of his boots. When he stepped back, the tingling stopped.

"Well," he said quietly. And shrugged. And moved again, swiveling about to check the seats, noting that the town itself couldn't be seen from down here.

The tingling returned.

He looked down as he walked, not knowing what to search for, but certain that whatever caused the

**81**

sensation came from beneath the large, close-fitting cobblestones.

An underground river, perhaps; its passage might cause the ground to tremble a bit. Maybe.

It wasn't unpleasant, simply disturbing.

At least not until he reached the center of the floor.

That's when he felt as if he'd been struck by one of his father's bolts of lightning.

There was a brief moment of agony; the world turned blinding white, and just as swiftly turned an unrelenting black through which he felt himself falling.

Dead, he cried silently; this is what it's like to be dead.

A good part of the reason Salmoneus felt that his scheme would be successful was the fact that he often allowed local talent to appear in the show. In the past this had proven to heighten community interest, add a few more paying bodies to the audience, and once, in the case of Delilah the Contortionist, actually provide him with a decent act he could invite to join the troupe.

The drawback was the auditions.

He had been at his table in the tavern since mid-morning, and it seemed as if half of Phyphe wanted to be in show business. With Virgil announcing each aspiring act, and Flovi in the corner providing accompaniment with a lyre and flute, he listened to breathless declamations, watched jugglers and mimes, braved a trained pig and a horse that was supposedly able to read minds, winced through enough songs to make his teeth ache, and suffered through a spectacularly bizarre performance by a guy who acted out highlights of Plato's *Dialogue* with himself.

But Salmoneus kept smiling, was unfailingly polite with each rejection, and couldn't help feeling as if his lips were going to fall off.

When the last person left, he sagged back in his chair and groaned.

"Pretty bad, huh?" Virgil said.

Salmoneus nodded wearily.

"Got to pick at least one more, though. In a hurry. The show starts in two hours."

Salmoneus nodded again. For purely pragmatic reasons, Olivia Stellas would be invited to read an epic poem she had written about the founding of Phyphe. To deny her would, Virgil had whispered, cause too many problems. As it was, the agreement Virgil had made with her and the other town leaders would barely produce a decent profit once the troupe's run was over. When she was finished, Salmoneus would be lucky not to have to give all the audience its money back.

As it was, his earlier hope that nothing would go wrong had been cruelly shattered when he had learned that a prominent family had been robbed the night before, mostly jewelry and loose money, nothing large, nothing heavy. As if that weren't bad enough, the husband had been struck with a club and still hadn't come around. And Hercules had cornered him just after breakfast, wanting to know about earthquakes or something.

A miracle, he prayed silently, with a pious glance to the tavern ceiling; nothing spectacular, but I could sure use one now.

At that moment a young woman strode into the room, planted herself in front of Salmoneus' table, and said, "I want to sing and be a star."

"Of course you do, my dear," Salmoneus responded kindly. She was a short, rather plain woman with close-cropped brown hair and a gently rounded figure from top to bottom, and she wore a certain pungent, familiar perfume he couldn't quite place. He tilted his head toward Flovi. "Just tell him what you're going to sing and he'll—"

"Sorry, but I work alone," she declared.

Salmoneus felt the smile begin to crack. "Whatever you want . . . uh . . ."

"Merta," she said.

"Lovely name."

"Lovely," Flovi whispered, loud enough for them to hear.

Merta glanced at him, looked back at Salmoneus, blinked once, and looked at Flovi again. "Do . . . do I know you?"

"No," Flovi answered wistfully.

"Oh."

"The song," Salmoneus prodded gently. He was hungry, and would barely have time to eat before the performance as it was. He'd give the little woman two notes, maybe three, before ending the session.

Merta took another long second before turning back to him. She clasped her hands loosely at her waist, swallowed nervously, and without introduction began to sing.

Salmoneus didn't recognize the melody, but he gave her a lot more than the allotted three notes. Especially when Flovi, unbidden, took up his flute and added a bittersweet background to her song. When she finished, Virgil sighed in appreciation while, at the same time, dabbing at his eyes with his sleeves.

Flovi simply gaped, the flute forgotten in his hands.

"That was . . ." Salmoneus wasn't quite sure what to say. It was lovely, to be sure; it was moving, without a doubt; yet something vital was missing. A resonance, perhaps, or a depth that he reckoned, that he prayed, might come with experience and training. "Good."

Merta stared. "Good? That's it? Even the jackass thinks I'm better than that."

"Hey," Flovi muttered.

"Not you," she snapped.

"All right—very good, then," Salmoneus allowed as he stood. Before she could protest, he was around the table and had a hand on her elbow. He told her on the way to the exit that he would be honored if she would sing the following night, that she should practice well and long without straining that voice, and that she should, under no circumstances, let anyone know how much he would pay her.

Merta stopped on the threshold. "Pay?" When she smiled, she was no longer plain. "Pay?"

"Pay," he said, and gave her a gentle shove outside. When she was gone, he turned to Virgil. "Two things."

"Name it," the young man said eagerly.

"First, be sure that woman shows up."

"Got it."

"I'll do it," Flovi volunteered, and was out of the tavern before either man could stop him.

Salmoneus shrugged. "Okay, now I eat."

"The second thing?" Virgil reminded him.

"Oh. Yes. Make sure that Olivia woman doesn't show up."

"What?"

"Virgil, she'll put everyone to sleep who hasn't already climbed over the walls if we let her go on. We'll be dead, broke, and ruined."

"She'll close us down if we do it."

Salmoneus smiled. "She likes you, son. Keep her happy."

Virgil paled.

Flovi ran back into the room. "You'd better come with me."

"Now what?" Salmoneus patted his stomach. "I haven't eaten all day. How can I—"

"Herc—" He glanced at Virgil. "Your strongman is dead."

"What?"

Flovi flapped a hand. "Okay, maybe he's not dead, but he's lying down in the middle of the arena, and he isn't moving."

Hercules heard hushed voices.

This, he thought sourly, is getting to be a habit.

After some effort his eyes fluttered open and squinted against the afternoon's light. He lay on his stomach, and as the voices expressed varying degrees of gratitude that he was still alive, he pushed himself up to his hands and knees. He braced himself for another shock, another plunge into the dark, then sat back on his heels, palms resting on his thighs.

He felt no tingling at all, and he seemed to be in one piece. No burns on his skin, no scorch marks on his clothing, nothing on the arm guards forged by Hephestus specially for him.

It was as if nothing had happened.

"Hercules?" Salmoneus stood in front of him, concern and puzzlement narrowing his eyes. "Are you all right?"

"Drunk," someone said.

Salmoneus glared over Hercules' head. "Don't be stupid, Virgil. He's not that sort. Now, get on with it. We have a show, remember?"

"I'm fine," Hercules said, pleased that his voice still worked. "I think."

Salmoneus held out a hand, and Hercules held it tightly as he pulled himself to his feet. "Strangest thing."

"What?"

Hercules looked around, seeing but paying no attention to several people standing at various points around the arena floor. "I don't know, really. It was like . . ." He frowned and shook his head. "Like a bolt."

"Lightning?" Salmoneus scanned the sky worriedly. "Oh my, not now, not before the show."

"Not a real bolt," Hercules said impatiently. He stared at the cobbles, bent over and brushed them with his fingertips.

Nothing.

"At least I don't think so."

Torn between concern for his friend and concern for losing his shirt if no one came to the show because of a storm, Salmoneus touched Hercules' arm. "Maybe you should lie down or something. You've been working awfully hard."

Right, Hercules thought; I've also been fighting bandits, getting drugged, sat on by a Harpy, and zapped by lightning that came out of the ground. Working too hard doesn't even begin to describe it.

He checked the cobblestones again.

Out of the ground.

"Salmoneus, has this ever happened before? To anyone else?"

"Here?"

"Anywhere. Anywhere that you've been."

"I don't know. I doubt it. I mean, I think I would know if any of my people were . . ." He stopped, one eye nearly closed in thought. "Dragar."

"Who?"

"Dragar, Hercules." Salmoneus rubbed his hands together slowly. "I heard him tell Aulma once that he'd gotten all tingly or something when he stepped into the arena at . . ." He closed both eyes. Shook his head. "I don't remember. I thought he was talking about the excitement of performing."

After a long silence Hercules said, "I'm sure he was, Salmoneus. I'm sure he was."

# 10

"So," Salmoneus said with a broad grin, "what do you think? Not bad, huh?"

Much to Hercules' surprise, it wasn't.

The arena was only half-filled, but those hundred or so adults and children seemed to be having a great time. Each of the dozen acts was greeted with warm applause, each performance cheered when it was over. Salmoneus acted as master of ceremonies, resplendent in a billowing gold robe, moving the performers on and off with practiced ease.

Delilah the Contortionist was amazing; a little man who told slightly ribald, humorous stories delighted the adults and puzzled the kids; Clova and Aeton were impressive as they performed intricate tumbling routines, and juggled everything from large balls to squealing piglets; and Flovi, when he wasn't playing with a local band as accompaniment to the performers, was wonderful as a flute soloist.

At the same time Virgil walked along the rows, a tray hanging from a strap around his neck, trying to sell snacks wrapped in ribbons. The problem was, the kids' hands were quicker than his ability to catch them.

He also looked incredibly tired.

"You're last," Salmoneus said with a slap to Hercules' shoulder as he ran out to introduce the next act.

Hercules smiled gamely.

He felt like an idiot.

In one of the caravan's chests his friend had discovered a great long cape made of wool, dyed a vivid red, and weighing at least as much as four grown men. The idea was to show himself briefly at the end while Salmoneus extolled the Power Beast's strength and ferocity, and dared the local strongmen to test themselves.

Hercules had complained that it wasn't fair, that no one knew who he really was, but all Salmoneus had done was wink and say, "Don't worry, I have a plan."

That was what he was afraid of.

He moved closer to the tunnel's end, watching the audience as much as the acts. He had spotted Peyra earlier, sitting in the front row on his left, but was unable to get her attention.

Hidden by the heavy thatch, both tunnels were deeply shadowed; so he was, in effect, invisible.

Dragar was the last act.

After an introduction usually reserved for kings and war heroes, the magician strolled out of the north tunnel behind Aulma, who wore a dark blue cloak over what appeared to be not much at all. It was difficult to tell because she seldom stopped moving. With the band's spirited help, she danced most of the time, spinning around the arena in her bare feet, the cape opening and closing in a deliberate tease.

Dragar himself remained in the center, in a simple black robe. The shepherd's crook had been replaced by a staff Hercules reckoned was at least six feet high, made of gleaming black wood twisted in a tight spiral.

Affixed to the top was a globe of silver almost as large as the head of a man. It was smoothly sculpted into the head of a ram, thick horns curving back from its skull into crescents that ended in obviously sharp points just ahead of its jaw.

They were made of gold.

The audience was enthralled.

Dragar pulled doves from his sleeves, ribbons from the hair of those sitting in the front row, and scarves from empty air; fire burned in his palms, rose in spinning balls hatched from eggs Aulma handed to him, and was sketched in the air when he spun the staff over his head; he had children climb down from their seats to act as his assistants, giving them coins for their reward and, each time, a brightly colored scarf or ribbon he pulled from their ears.

He said not a word.

He let his magic speak for him.

And when he finished, the crowd came to its feet and cheered itself hoarse.

As the magician strode from the arena without acknowledging the response, Hercules realized that he, too, was applauding, and he didn't stop until he spotted Peyra again. She was on her feet with the others, but her face was pale, her lips bloodless, and her hands were folded protectively over her stomach.

She looked as if she had seen a ghost.

Suddenly Salmoneus was at Hercules' side, tugging at his arm.

"Come on, Beast, you're on."

Before Hercules knew it, he was in the open, keeping his head down as Salmoneus began his pitch. A few laughed, a few hooted, and he could also hear several distinct growls of *He don't look so strong.*

Thank the gods, he thought, Iolaus isn't here; I'd never live this down.

The band played raucously, and Salmoneus spread his arms and announced that for tomorrow's performance, the mighty Red Power Beast would bend an iron bar with his bare hands.

Hercules stared at him.

The crowd didn't believe it. Loudly.

"Okay," Salmoneus said with a laugh. "You're right, ladies and gentlemen, that's too easy for the Beast. How about breaking a timber over his head?"

The stare became a glare.

The crowd laughed.

Undeterred by the skepticism, Salmoneus suggested lifting an ox with one hand, hefting a wagon, or breaking a tree in half. He would have gone on, but Hercules had had enough. He flipped the cape back over his shoulders, grabbed Salmoneus by his belt with one hand, and with a humorless grin, lifted him effortlessly over his head.

"Hey!" Salmoneus yelped, arms waving, feet kicking. "Hey, wait a minute!"

The crowd cheered, the band played, the crowd left, and Salmoneus said, "You can let me down now."

Hercules looked up at him. "Break a timber over my head?"

Salmoneus instantly held out his palms. "Just a thought, just a thought. So they'll know you're strong, you see?"

"I think we've covered that now."

Salmoneus closed his eyes tightly and groaned. "I think I'm getting air sick."

A voice called Hercules then, and he saw Peyra standing at the south tunnel.

He started over.

"Hey!" Salmoneus said.

Without looking, Hercules opened his fingers and kept moving, enjoying the sound of Salmoneus landing hard on his feet, then harder on his rump. He unbuckled the ludicrous cape and tossed it aside, took Peyra's arm, and said, "Let's go for a walk."

"But Hercules, it's—"

"Not here," he told her. "Later. When we're alone."

"It's him," she said dully, her hands twisting in her lap. "I'd know him anywhere."

They sat on the grassy bank of the waterfall pond, hunched against the growing twilight.

Hercules plucked a handful of grass from between his legs and, after staring at it for a moment, scattered it over the water. "He's very good at what he does."

She looked at him expressionlessly. "You still don't believe me."

"I've seen magicians before, Peyra. Some not as good as Dragar, some better. It's all tricks and illusions, not real magic at all. Aulma and all that dancing—all she did was distract the people from looking too closely at what Dragar was doing." He paused as he watched the blades of grass spin with the current. "But I have to admit that I'm not as sure of that as I used to be."

She said nothing.

A bird called softly in the trees behind them, and they were far enough from the waterfall to hear the occasional croaking of a bullfrog and the splash of a fish.

"So what do we do now?" she wanted to know.

He scratched through his hair from back to front, frowned, and finally shrugged with one shoulder. "I need to talk to him, I guess. I need . . ." He inhaled deeply, let the breath out slowly. "I need to be sure."

"Then what?"

"Then I suppose I need to do something about it."

"Like what?"

"I don't know."

"Why?"

"I haven't gotten that far."

"Why?"

He looked at her. "You know, you sure do ask an awful lot of questions that I don't have answers to."

"I do?"

He grinned, and she giggled. "Sorry." Then, sobering quickly, she took light hold of his arm. "Just be careful, all right? I don't want him turning you into a frog, too." Before he could answer, she leaned over and kissed him on the cheek, blushed, and scrambled to her feet. "I'd better go. Agatra will be worried."

As she made her way back toward the path, he watched and wondered if the Harpy's cave suited her. Then he wondered what he would do next. Talk to Dragar, obviously, although he knew it wouldn't do much good. The magician would hardly admit to possessing such skills. And, even if he did, it was no crime.

It was what the man intended to do with the skills that Hercules needed to know.

He tossed another handful of grass into the pond, stretched, and decided he might as well head back. Twilight had hazed the air, and the overcast sky was already dark. A cloud of gnats danced over the water's surface; from the shallows fish leapt for their evening meal.

He heard the cry just as he stood.

Frowning he hurried toward the path, stepping around a bush in time to see Peyra being dragged into the woods by a man in dark clothing.

Hercules ran, swerving into the trees before he

reached the two figures. The man made no attempt to cover Peyra's mouth; he had one arm around her waist and half-dragged her along, ignoring the flailing blows from her hands and feet.

"Hey!" Hercules called.

Peyra screamed.

The man didn't stop, even though it was obvious he wasn't going to get very far.

Hercules reached them in seconds, grabbed the man's shoulder, and, at the same time, realized what he gotten himself into.

Uh-oh, he thought when something hard slammed into the back of his left leg.

A streak of fire raced from his thigh to his shoulder, and he fell onto his back, gasping in pain. Suddenly a huge knobbed club swept out of the dark. He managed to roll aside just a split-second before it would have crushed his skull.

There was no time for relief—the club tried again, and he rolled to his right this time, and lashed out with one foot. He missed the assailant, but the club missed his head and he was able to spring to his feet.

Peyra was on the ground not twenty feet away, keening in fear, with her arms tucked over her head protectively, her legs drawn up to her chest.

The trees here were tall, the lowest branches high and thin, and the air was more like dusk than by the water, like looking through a black-speckled veil. There were only a few low shrubs, nothing Hercules could see that could be used as a weapon.

Which was too bad, because there were four of

them, all wearing dark brown clothes with knee-high boots, all carrying thick, knobbed clubs.

He was surrounded, turning slowly to try to keep all of them in sight at the same time, looking for the weak link, the one who seemed the most nervous or the least comfortable with his weapon.

There wasn't one.

"Nuts," he muttered when they all charged at once.

# 11

The rules of engagement in a situation like this were simple: if the enemy is organized, well armed, and clearly motivated toward mayhem, run until you can figure out what to do next; if the enemy is disorganized, armed but not heavily, and even the slightest bit uncertain, stick around and fight; and if the enemy is armed but obviously much too confident in its ability to bring down the target, use that confidence to even the odds as much as you can.

Hercules had no intention of running.

He picked the man facing him and met charge with charge, ducking under the swinging club, and straightening as he cupped a hand under the man's jaw. He lifted and turned and threw, hoping to take at least one of the others out.

He didn't.

The thrown man pinwheeled harmlessly over their heads and, amazingly enough, landed lightly on his feet. Meanwhile, a blow stunned Hercules' left shoulder just as he parried another with his arm guard. That blow stung his arm as well, and he couldn't help it—he dropped to one knee and shook his head quickly to clear it.

Not quickly enough.

A club landed solidly across his shoulders, driving him to both knees. He grabbed an ankle in front of him and yanked, toppling the attacker. As a third blow caught his back without much force, he dragged the struggling man to him and snatched his club away.

"Ha," he said.

"Ha, yourself," a familiar voice answered, and whacked his wrist, sending the captured club spinning out of reach.

This is not going well, he thought, and launched himself backward, colliding with the man just behind him. But the man didn't fall; he just danced to one side until he regained his balance.

A club bashed the ground beside Hercules' chest. He rolled out of the way of two more blows, came up against a bush, and used it to pull himself shakily to his feet.

One of the men grinned at him, the gap between his front teeth visible even in the dusky light.

"You," Hercules said.

Sid nodded. "That's right." His grin widened. "You remember my brother Chicus, I suppose?"

Hercules didn't look; he ducked, and the breeze of a passing club ruffled his hair.

When he straightened, he was surrounded again.

"This is a little different than robbing wagons," he said. "Or drugging people."

"More fun," Chicus answered from his right.

Sid tapped his club on the ground. "No more talking, big man. We talk, you look for a way out, we get lulled into not thinking clearly, and you get away. Or hurt us." The gap seemed to widen. "Not this time."

Hercules glared; the man knew too many rules himself.

Sid raised his weapon, a signal to ready the next charge, and Hercules braced himself. His only hope was, again, to concentrate on one of them, get his club, and even matters up.

The obvious target was Sid.

Sid knew it. He winked, lost the grin, and brought the club down—

Just as a hoarse, lingering, unearthly cry tore through the forest and froze them all.

"What in—?" Chicus said nervously.

The horrid cry sounded again, this time from directly overhead, and before any of them could move, a large dark shape exploded out of the high branches. One of the men shrieked in terror, brandished his club, and shrieked again when Agatra snared the cloth at his shoulders with her talons and began to carry him away.

Evidently, however, the man weighed more than she had bargained for. He was also busy flailing and thrashing and kicking and wriggling. As a result, she wasn't able to gain much altitude, nor was she able to move in a straight line.

Struggling to maintain control, she veered too close to a tree and the bandit thumped against the bole, yelped in pain, thumped against the next one, yelped, and continued in a succession of veering, thumping, and yelping until they were out of sight.

"Sid," Chicus said, his voice nearly squeaking in fear as he exchanged wide-eyed glances with the third man. "Sid, we—"

"Shut up," Sid snapped, squinting in the direction his man had gone.

"But—"

"I said—"

He didn't finish.

He couldn't.

Hercules stood directly in front of him, one hand on his club wrist, the other gathering a fistful of shirt.

Hercules smiled.

Sid winced.

This time Hercules checked over his shoulder, saw the other two stumbling toward him, and aimed as he lifted, turned, and tossed, following up on the throw by running after Sid in hopes of liberating one of those clubs. By the time Sid reached the ground, however, Chicus and the other man were gone, stepping nimbly to one side to allow their leader an unceremonious landing on the very large exposed roots of a very large tree.

You guys are fast, Hercules thought, and jumped back from a swinging club, jumped back again, and would have been forced to dodge a third time had it not been for Agatra's return.

She hovered over them, sending the third man into a frenzy of club swinging and eerily silent dodging, while Chicus darted out of the way and pulled Sid to his feet.

"Enough," Sid snarled.

Hercules agreed.

He strode toward them, staring, not flinching when Chicus raised his weapon, not blinking when Sid growled, howled in frustration and rage, and charged.

Hercules took the club's blow on his right arm, grabbed Sid's shoulder with his left hand and flipped him onto his back, then stepped over and caught Chicus' club on its way down.

For a moment they froze as Chicus strained to free his weapon, but he soon realized the futility of it, and smiled wanly before letting go and spinning around to run.

Hercules tapped him on the head. With the club.

Chicus hunched his shoulders, staggered one more step, and collapsed.

But not before Sid, in a move born of the desperation of a man who just couldn't catch a break, wrapped his arms around Hercules' leg and tried to pull him down.

"Oh, please," Hercules said.

Sid growled, squirmed, and managed to coil himself around the other leg.

"Hercules?"

He looked around until he saw Peyra, sitting up and frowning.

"Are you all right?" she asked, puzzled.

He looked down while Sid tried to bite through his boots. "Sure."

"I thought I heard Agatra. Where is . . .?"

Hercules had completely forgotten about the remaining bandit. As best he could, with Sid snarling and gnawing on his boot, he turned, grinned, and pointed. "There."

Agatra had somehow wrenched the club from Sid's last man, and now hovered above him, doing her best to beat him senseless. The problem seemed to be one of coordination and skill—she was not used to using both wings and arms simultaneously, and her swings were vicious but wildly off the mark, each one sending her into a spin that, at one point, had her flying upside down.

The bandit was too terrified to notice the advantage he'd been given; he raced from one tree to another, arms wrapped over his head, moaning entreaties to the gods for protection.

"Will you hold still?" she yelled.

The bandit, who may have been terrified but wasn't stupid, didn't. He didn't stop praying either.

She grunted and swung. Missed. Spun. Grunted and swung. And began to wobble a little.

Hercules realized she was making herself dizzy.

He also realized that Peyra had drawn up her legs and cupped her hands around her knees. Bemused, she watched the Harpy, then watched Sid, then watched the Harpy again. Hercules had a feeling this whole affair somehow didn't quite live up to the battle stories she had listened to around the village campfire.

It was about this time that Agatra's bandit finally understood that luck was on his side for a change.

When Agatra swung, and missed, and hung upside down cursing, he took off into the woods. Not long after that, Hercules decided it was time to do something about Sid; he looked down, and grunted when he saw that his legs were unencumbered—the bandit leader was gone, and so was Chicus.

The evening was silent.

Not even the sound of running footsteps.

"You know," Peyra said with a shake of her head, "I simply had no idea."

Nightfall was complete.

After making sure Peyra would be able to handle a woozy Agatra and get her back to the cave, Hercules strode angrily toward Phyphe, a switch in one hand whipping every shrub and bole he passed.

The switch didn't last very long.

Neither did the anger; it soon passed into disgust.

He had been a fool, and he was not only disgusted at himself, he felt like a complete idiot for being so blind. The attack on Peyra had obviously been a trap set to lure him in. Not to kill him, but to stall him. Had Sid and his three cronies really wanted him to die, they would have used swords, or worse. They may have been hard men, but they weren't the kind who would bludgeon a man to death.

Something was up in town, he knew it, and he suspected he was far too late to stop it.

It was, he figured, another robbery.

Viciously he kicked a rock in his way, sending it whistling through the night until it buried itself in the bole of a black-bark oak.

"Jerk," he muttered. "Fool."

When he reached the road and headed for town, he calmed down enough to understand that it wasn't just tonight that bothered him. It was everything.

From the very beginning he hadn't taken Salmoneus' problems all that seriously. Salmoneus was part of the problem, of course, simply by being Salmoneus, but that was no excuse.

He should have known there was something else going on, something besides the minor disasters that had beset the Traveling Theater of Fun. After all, hints and clues had been throwing themselves in his way ever since he'd first arrived, and all he had done was trample them without thinking.

That wasn't like him.

It wasn't like him to slough off being drugged; it wasn't like him not to pursue the odd tremors he'd felt in the middle of the night; it wasn't like him to ignore what had happened in the arena today.

Nothing he had done was like him at all.

It was almost as if Circe or one of the Sirens had cast one of their enchantments, blinding him to the truth without him realizing it.

Making him complacent.

It was . . .

He stopped, blinked, and whacked his forehead with the heel of one hand.

It was like . . . magic.

A full minute passed before he began to smile.

Well, he thought, I guess it's time I did something about it.

And since strangling Salmoneus for getting him into this was out of the question, he would start with the reason he had been lured into tonight's trap.

The reason, and the person behind it.

# 12

Phyphe had no actual protective wall. Because of its circular construction, the sides and backs of its outer buildings served the same purpose. As a result, there were four primary entrances to the town itself, each flanked by thick, ten-foot-high poles; atop the poles were torches that burned from dusk to dawn.

Salmoneus stood just outside the north entrance, staring glumly at his flickering shadow. He knew that out there in the dark were a scattering of trees and the fields that supplied Phyphe with its crops and cattle. A simple life. A life that had no room for a man of real vision.

He sighed.

He scratched his beard.

He took a few steps up the road and squinted, trying to force a vision out of the dim shapes the torchlight created. What he wanted was a sign that vaudalville was really going to work. That he had really hit the Big Vision this time.

What he got was a headache.

He also got the distinct impression that the earth was about to move.

He turned slowly, holding his breath as he licked his lips nervously.

He could see farther down the street than he could up the road, because several businesses along the way had lanterns burning above their doorways. The street was empty, not even the shadow of a scrounging mongrel or prowling cat.

A glance up at the torches; they burned steadily, without a breeze to twist them.

He rubbed his eyes with the heels of his hands. He was tired, that's all. It took a lot of work to pull something like vaudalville together time after time. A lot of work to keep his performers from tearing each other's throats out when they thought he was favoring one over another. A lot of work searching for the one act, the one person, the one performing genius that would make his fortune.

At first he had believed that person was Dragar. Although the man acted like a bumbling fool most of the time, once he was in front of an audience he was transformed. But you could only pull so many ribbons from a kid's ear, so many fireballs from the palm of a hand, before people became bored and wanted to see more.

Now that Merta woman, she had promise. If only he could figure out what she lacked. She wasn't gorgeous, not like Aulma, although she was attractive enough; she wasn't flashy, not like Delilah, but she seemed to have presence. It's just that she wasn't . . . quite . . . right.

Hercules, of course, could easily be that Big Act, but it wouldn't happen. He didn't have show business in his blood, not like Salmoneus. That wasn't a bad thing; it just wasn't going to make his fortune.

He sighed aloud and decided he might as well get on to bed. He had another busy day tomorrow, and needed all the rest he could get.

But he didn't move.

The feeling hadn't left.

Again he looked around and saw nothing; again he checked the sky and saw nothing.

Now he wished Hercules was with him. Demigods had a way of sensing things, and Hercules was better than most. Even if he didn't appreciate the genius behind the concept of the Red Power Beast.

Demigods may be demigods, but they didn't always have vision.

His own, latest vision was that if he took one step, then whatever was about to happen would happen. So all he had to do was stand here for a while, and it, whatever *it* was, would get tired of waiting and go away.

Demigods didn't think that way.

So, as slowly as he could without giving himself cramps, he settled cross-legged in the middle of the road, arranged the hem of his robe demurely around his shins, and waited.

Virgil stumbled out of the darkened house, stumbled down the street toward the inn where he was staying, and nearly fell when his right leg decided it didn't really want to work anymore.

He was exhausted.

He had had no idea being Salmoneus' road manager entailed so much work besides managing. Every other muscle ached, and the muscles that didn't ache felt as if they had turned to water.

He was young and reasonably healthy, but at this rate, keeping Olivia Stellas out of the arena was going to turn him into an old man before the end of the week.

If it didn't kill him first.

He turned a corner blindly, and collided with someone, who cursed and shoved him hard into a wall before hurrying away.

"Hey," he said, "watch where you're going." He rubbed the back of his head gingerly. "Drunk."

Before he could take another step, however, someone else ran into him. As he fell back he reached out to grab the man, caught only a piece of sleeve, and was slammed into the wall again.

This time the "Hey" was rather feeble, since the back of his skull hit the stone harder. In fact, the force of the collision finished doing to his legs what Olivia had started—they stopped functioning completely, and he slid dazed to the ground.

"Vaudalville," he said grumpily to the empty street, "sucks."

But he didn't try to get up.

On top of everything else, he had the clear impression that any movement on his part would cause something worse than a couple of collisions with a couple of drunks. So he sat there, humming quietly, waiting for the stars that danced in front of him to go away.

Flovi didn't know what to say, and so he said nothing.

Merta didn't know what to say, and so she blathered and babbled and felt a fierce blush set fire to her cheeks.

They had worked most of the evening outside the stable, Flovi with his flute, she with her considerable knowledge of songs both local and from parts of the world Flovi had never even heard of. They knew from the first note that they complemented each other well; yet they also sensed there was something not quite right with what they did.

Finally, although they were pleased with the way they sounded, that missing "something" frustrated them into a silence that lasted until Flovi's stomach growled. That produced a round of giggles, some pleasant embarrassment, and a leisurely meal at the nearest tavern, during which they traded dreams and lives. And a few lies to make them sound better.

Eventually the dinner had to end.

Flovi, being the gentleman, offered to walk Merta home.

Merta, not being stupid, accepted.

The silence returned when they reached the door of her home, broken when Merta couldn't stand it any longer. She had no idea what to say, and so said it at length, thinking that sooner or later he would stop her. Preferably with a kiss. She had a feeling that his mustache would tickle, and she looked forward to it with an intensity that took her breath away.

And, not coincidentally, shut her up.

"Uh," Flovi said.

Merta smiled. He was cute. A little mature for someone of her age, but definitely cute.

"You see," Flovi said, staring wildly at the door, the windows, the roof, the street.

Merta, who realized that this was almost exactly like getting the stupid jackass out of its stall when all it wanted to do was sleep and eat, took his hand.

Flovi swallowed.

"I know you're new in town," she said, suddenly unable to meet his gaze, "but it's customary in Phyphe for a young man to bestow a good evening kiss on a young woman, especially when the young man has spent all day with the young woman working hard to perfect the young woman's musical skills. For which assistance, it goes without saying, the young woman is very, very grateful." She looked and smiled. "It beats mucking out the stables any day."

To her relief he grinned.

To her astonishment, and delight, he leaned down and kissed her lightly on the lips.

"Oh, my," she said breathlessly.

"You . . . felt it?"

She nodded. "It almost moved, didn't it?"

At which point they realized that this wasn't exactly the stage of the game where the earth was, in fact, supposed to move. It wasn't, in fact, supposed to do much of anything.

"What is it?" she whispered fearfully.

He shook his head; he didn't know.

Neither did she, but she was positive that if either of them moved, the earth, in fact, would, too.

Not exactly, Merta thought, the way I'd planned it.


Aulma knew she was often foolish, but did not believe she was a fool. When Dragar picked her to be his assistant, she understood immediately that he had no intention of letting his emotions get in the way of what he kept calling his ultimate plan.

Whatever that was.

And nothing since had changed that.

Oh, sure, they embraced once in a while, and he had even allowed her to kiss him one night after a particularly brilliant performance in a small town not far from Sparta. But that had been it. Even popping into his room stark naked had no effect—except to make her feel like a complete idiot.

She ought not to complain. She had volunteered for the position because she wanted out of her village. It was a nice place, but dull. Boring. Stultifying. She had traveled, she had seen excitement, she had eaten foods and had drinks she'd never known existed.

But she had never been truly afraid before.

Dragar had changed.

He had always been a little unnerving; now he was downright scary.

Tonight she walked the streets of Phyphe alone, unusually contemplative, wondering if maybe she ought to tell someone what she knew. The problem was, she really didn't know exactly what she knew. She just knew that she knew it. And if she could only figure out what it was that she knew, exactly, then maybe she could figure out if she should tell someone what she knew. Whatever that was.

She stopped.

She fanned herself with one hand.

She took a deep breath and ordered herself to stop thinking like that or she'd knock herself out. At that moment two men raced past her, nearly knocking her over, and she opened her mouth to yell at them. She changed her mind when they vanished into the shadows. Instead she headed back toward the inn, thinking Dragar wouldn't like it if he found out she had left.

She nearly tripped over a pair of legs sticking out of a wall.

"Hey," a voice said weakly. "Watch it, okay?"

"Virgil?" She leaned forward, peering into the shadows. "Virgil, is that you? Are you drunk?"

"Yes, it's me, and no, I'm not drunk. I've been run over by a herd of cattle."

She crouched at his feet. "Those two guys?"

"Okay, two guys. Doesn't matter. I'm in pain."

Her smile surprised her. Usually she paid no attention to him except to order him around at Dragar's command. She had gotten used it, kind of liked it, and now, inexplicably, felt mildly ashamed.

"Come on," she said, holding out her hand. "Let's get back. It'll be dawn in a couple of hours."

"No."

"Why not?"

His voice changed. "Aulma, can't you feel it?"

She frowned. "Feel what?"

"Hush."

She did, tilting her head as though that would help her figure out what he meant.

It did.

"Uh-oh," she said.

And Virgil said, "You got it."


Back at his room, Hercules sat up suddenly.

It was dark; no light came through the window.

"Oh, boy," he said.


In another room bathed with green light, someone said, "Oops."


And the earth *moved*.

# 13

It wasn't a quake or a tremor; the ground didn't roll or buck or twist or split apart.

Hercules felt as if he were standing on a table, and someone had decided to move it an inch or two across the room. The shift dumped him out of bed, and he braced himself for the collapse of the ceiling, the floor, the entire building.

Nothing happened.

He waited a few seconds more, reminded himself to start breathing again, and hurried to the window. Behind him he could hear the startled cries of others who had fallen; outside, a few people milled around in the street, pointing in every direction except down and speculating at the tops of their voices that some-one, somewhere, had screwed up a rite and one of the gods was ticked. As usual.

I don't think so, Hercules thought.

He watched for a while longer, but trouble seemed to be the last thing on those people's minds. They talked, they complained, they picked up a few fallen lanterns and pieces of roof, and one by one vanished into the night, leaving nothing but silence behind.

Still, he kept watch.

Five minutes later, two figures clad in black raced up the street and darted around a corner. He debated following, if only to confirm what he already suspected, then decided it wouldn't be worth it. Not yet. What he needed was more proof, and for that he would have to speak to Salmoneus first. After tonight, though, he didn't think the man would be in any condition to do anything but babble.

He grunted and returned to his bed.

You know, he said wordlessly to the ceiling, if anyone else were involved, this would be pretty straightforward. No complications like Harpies, magic, yellow frogs, Red Power Beasts, earthquakes that don't quake, and a tankard of drugged mead that wasn't all that good in the first place.

Just a simple matter of getting the goods on a burglar who thinks he's uncatchable.

No big deal.

But no . . . He had Salmoneus, and nothing, ever, was straightforward with Salmoneus.

On the other hand, life with Salmoneus wasn't ever dull, either. Or predictable.

Maybe, he thought, it would—

Something touched his shoulder. "Are you going to sleep all day?" Hercules opened his eyes, closed his eyes, opened his eyes again and grinned. "I was just thinking about you."

"You were snoring."

It was then that he realized the room was filled

with sunlight, he was hungry, and Salmoneus was as pale as the moon. He sat up, stretched, and told his friend that nothing was so important that it couldn't wait until after he had had a healthy breakfast.

"There isn't that much food in town," Salmoneus grumbled as they went downstairs.

Hercules shrugged. He ate. He listened as the other diners talked about the previous night, how unnerved they were, and how uncertain their futures were in a world where the gods played games with the very earth itself. They also complained darkly about those who took advantage of such terrible things, breaking into homes and stealing from those who were already frozen with fear. He gathered that the feeling was the same all over town, and it occurred to him that perhaps what had happened might actually work in his favor.

Assuming he was right.

When he finished his meal, he suggested to an impatient Salmoneus that he had a good idea why the more ordinary disasters had attached themselves to the traveling show.

Salmoneus snorted.

Hercules explained.

Salmoneus leaned far back in his chair and stared at the rafters until the chair fell over. Then he set the chair right, sat, and folded his hands across his paunch and twiddled his thumbs. "You're out of your mind. No offense, Hercules, but that's—"

"Impossible?"

"Of course."

"Why?"

Salmoneus tugged at his beard. "I don't know. Because things like that don't happen to me, I guess."

Hercules laughed. "Salmoneus, things like that happen to you all the time."

"Okay, but still—"

"I'll prove it to you tonight, after the show."

Surprisingly, Salmoneus shook his head sadly. "I don't know if there will be a show, Hercules. Not after what happened last night." He jerked a thumb over one shoulder. "I don't think they'll be in the mood."

Not good, Hercules thought; not good.

"Listen—"

Salmoneus waved a hand. "No, don't even try. I know you're upset with what I made you do, and I'm sorry. I guess I should have known better."

"What you made me do?"

"The Red Power Beast."

"Oh. Well—"

"I think maybe I'll just cut my losses—as we say in the business—and move on." He sighed so heavily the table almost shook. "If, that is, there's anyplace to move on to."

Worse than not good, Hercules realized; it was a disaster.

"Salmoneus, don't be silly." He reached across the table and poked his finger in the man's chest. "You, my friend, are *exactly* what this town needs after last night."

"What?"

Hercules nodded excitedly. "A diversion, Salmoneus. Don't you get it? A way to make them feel good again. And only you can provide it."

"Oh." Salmoneus rubbed a temple thoughtfully. "I hadn't thought of it that way."

"It's the only way to think about it."

It took a few seconds, but Salmoneus finally smiled.

"Good. Now, get on out there, friend, and put together the best darn show you can. The people of Phyphe need you."

Salmoneus leapt to his feet, saluted, laughed, and practically sprinted from the inn.

Hercules was horrified. By the gods, he thought with a shudder, I'm actually starting to sound like him.

He shuddered again, hoped he wasn't making a mistake, and asked the innkeeper where a man, or men, with little money might find places to stay.

The innkeeper, by the insulted look on his face, suggested that Phyphe had no places like that. It was a decent town. At least until those show business people came around.

Hercules, by a tilt of his head and a gesture, agreed that Phyphe was indeed a decent town, a great town, but even a great town, man to man, had places like that, even if no one liked to speak about it in public.

The innkeeper, reluctantly, admitted that yes, Phyphe, for all its greatness, might have a place like that. He just didn't remember offhand where it might be.

Hercules saw the discreet, outstretched palm.

The innkeeper saw the look on Hercules' face, saw the loosely clenched fist at Hercules' side, and saw the way Hercules' muscles bulged a little, which made them approximately larger than most of his body.

The outstretched palm withdrew, and was replaced by a finger that sketched a quick map on the tabletop.

Hercules thanked him.

The innkeeper told him it was no problem, glad to help a fellow out, especially one who spent fortunes on the kind of meals one found in a place like this.

Hercules got out before he got confused.

Less than an hour later, he reached his destination.

It was an inn in only the loosest sense of the word—so disreputable and grungy it didn't bother with a name. Which was pretty much the best way to describe the neighborhood as well.

When Hercules stepped inside and paused, waiting for his eyes to adjust to the dimness, he heard muttering and grumbling from a half dozen patrons at the tables scattered around the large room. He also heard a gasp off in the far corner to his right, followed quickly by another.

The bartender, a burly giant, ominously tapped a large club against his palm. "You got business here, friend?"

Hercules walked over, plucked the club from the bartender's hand, broke it in half over his thigh, smiled to mask the sudden pain in his leg, and said, "Yep."

The bartender smiled back gamely. "Good. Otherwise I would have to ask you to leave the premises."

"Good," Hercules said. He dropped the two halves of the club onto the bar, changed his mind, grabbed one of them, and walked over to the corner.

The four men at the table hadn't moved. "Gentlemen," he said pleasantly, "if I bought you all a drink, you probably still wouldn't want to talk to me peacefully, would you?"

Sid snickered; Chicus chortled; the mute one grunted derisively; the good-looking one, who also had more brains than his friends, held up his hands to indicate that he would sing like a bird if only he could leave with his bones intact. Preferably with them still on the inside of his skin.

"Hey," a voice said over Hercules' left shoulder, "you leave my buddies alone, creep."

Hercules didn't look around. He snapped his left arm up at the elbow and caught the man square on the nose with his fist. A grunt. A thud. A scraping back of chairs and the shuffling of booted feet hurrying toward the exit.

Hercules smiled and shrugged. "Manners," he said to no one in particular. "It all comes down to manners."

He pressed his hands against the table and leaned forward, forcing each of the bandits in turn to meet his gaze. "Are we talking?"

Chicus glanced toward the rafters. "You got that monster with you?"

"Maybe."

The mute one's lips began to quiver.

"The thing is," Hercules said, "if you answer my questions, and convince me you're not lying, nobody gets hurt and we all go home. If you lie . . ." He stared at the piece of club in his right hand, waited until he was sure they were looking, too, and squeezed.

Sid snickered; Chicus snorted derisively; the mute's lips quivered; the handsome one rolled his eyes in preparation for a faint.

And the piece of club shattered into sawdust.

Hercules shook his head and brushed the debris to the floor—smiling, shaking his head as if to say that sometimes he even amazed himself.

"Well?"

Sid snickered; Chicus smacked him on the arm; the mute leaned over and smacked his brother on the other arm; the handsome one's face began to lose its color.

"What do you want to know?" Chicus asked, doing his best to keep his image tough while, at the same time, making sure Hercules knew that cooperation was very much a part of the conversation.

"Which one of you drugged my drink the other night?"

None of them answered.

Hercules reached down, grabbed a handful of sawdust, and poured it into a pile on the table. He stared at it pointedly.

"Lutus," Chicus said quickly, and pointed at the mute.

"Good." He brushed some of the sawdust away. "Who are you working for?"

"What?" Chicus sounded insulted. "We're our own gang!"

"Who," Hercules repeated slowly, "are you working for?"

Sid growled a *shut up* when Chicus opened his mouth to answer, and Lutus went almost as pale as his brother.

Hercules had just about run out of patience. He rose to his full height, paid no attention when the handsome one fainted off his chair, and slammed a fist onto the table. Which split in half.

"Who paid you to drug me?" he demanded. "Who paid you to keep me out of town last night? And," he added, glaring right at Chicus, "have you told him who I am?"

Lutus' hands sprang into action, weaving a pattern so complex it nearly crossed Hercules' eyes. Oddly enough, he understood some of it—the part that assured him they had said nothing to anyone about who he really was.

For no reason at all Hercules believed him.

"Well?" he said to Sid. "What did he say?"

"He said mind your own flamin' business," Sid sneered.

"That's it," he said wearily. He reached over and snatched Sid out of his chair, held him up until they were nose-to-nose, and said, "One more useless answer, *friend,* and I'll give you to my feathered friend."

That did it.

Sid told him.

Hercules dropped him onto the wreckage of the table, dusted his palms, and suggested that they, having now become rather unreliable in terms of their employer, might find it healthier to seek employment somewhere else. Somewhere else far, far away.

"Can I pack?" Chicus asked. "I've picked up these really swell—"

Hercules stared.

Chicus and Lutus immediately picked up their unconscious brother and hustled from the inn. Sid, after some face-saving posturing that included kicking a lot of sawdust around, ended up only a half step behind them.

By the time Hercules reached the street, all the gang had left behind was a lingering cloud of dust.

One down, one to go, he thought, and headed for the arena.

He had nearly reached it when he heard a woman scream.

# 14

She stood in front of an elegant house whose portal was flanked by modestly ornate pillars, whose marble lintel was carved into delicate swirls of grape leaves and roses, and whose walls were decorated with hideous green triangular designs.

No one stood near her. In fact, no one stood within a hundred feet of her. Yet a crowd had gathered nonetheless, and when Hercules pushed his way through, all he saw was a woman whose deep black hair had fallen loose of its coils, whose belted robe matched the green tiles, and whose richly sandaled feet stomped the marble stoop in time to her shrieks.

Curious, he moved toward her, wondering why none of the others had offered to help.

She shrieked, she stomped, she looked at him and said, "Who . . . are . . . you?"

He began to understand. "I'm—" He caught himself just in time, and managed to cover by muttering that he worked with the Salmoneus vaudalville troupe, had heard her distress, and wanted to offer his services. If he could.

She folded her hands arrogantly at her waist. "Are you trained in the recovery of valuable jewels?"

He admitted as how he wasn't, not really.

"Are you skilled in the tracking of dastardly criminals who have sullied my home simply by breathing the same air as I?"

"No," he said.

"Then you are of no use to me."

She shrieked.

He shrugged and walked away, stopping only when she called to him—as someone might call a particularly filthy, but faithful, dog.

He looked over his shoulder.

"Virgil," she said, pursing her thick red lips. "Virgil?"

She stared haughtily at him for a moment before nodding. "Ah. You're the strongman."

The way she said it indicated that strength, in her opinion, equaled severely diminished brain power.

It was all he could do just to nod.

"Virgil is one of your employers, young man," she said, managing to look down at him without coming anywhere near his height. "Do tell him that Olivia Stellas requires his presence immediately."

And she shrieked.

Hercules wondered how much trouble he could get into with how many gods if he popped her one, decided it wasn't worth finding out, and made his way back down the street. He did not head for the arena, however. He went directly to the Gold Leaf

Inn, which he found on a quiet street filled primarily with the kind of shops only someone like Olivia Stellas would frequent.

It was, he thought, a curious place for a simple vaudalville act to stay. Especially one that didn't receive very large compensation.

The innkeeper, a woman of airs nearly as rarefied as Olivia's, took one look at him and tried to shoo him away. Took another look and decided he was worth looking at a third time—so boldly that Hercules almost checked to be sure he still had his clothes on.

When he spoke, she nearly swooned; when he requested permission to visit one of her guests, she simpered, as well as anyone he had ever seen, without actually groveling; when she suggested none too coyly that he visit her before he left, his response was a noncommittal shrug that made her grab weakly for the nearest chair.

Weird, he thought as he took the stairs to the second floor two at a time; weird, and dangerous.

He found the right door he needed without any trouble. Nor did he have any trouble getting in, because he didn't bother to knock; he just pushed the door open and stepped over the threshold.

Clova Junarus, wearing a snug tunic and sitting on a low bench in front of a polished copper mirror, didn't jump, didn't flinch, didn't yell. She stared at him, scowled, and called, "Aeton, that creature is here."

From the next room, Aeton called, "What creature?"

"Me," Hercules said.

Aeton appeared in the doorway, drying his hands on a long white cloth. Other than that, he was pretty much naked. "Oh. You. What do you want?"

"Oh, do get dressed, Aeton," Clova said wearily.

Aeton shrugged, tossed the cloth over his shoulder, and left.

Clova sighed the sigh of one who had too many responsibilities and none of the glory. "What do you want?"

Hercules walked over to the table beneath the mirror, reached over her shoulder, and picked up a necklace of red and green gems set in silver blossoms. "Very nice. You two are married, right? Not brother and sister."

"Right." She snatched it away. "Beast."

"That's me."

Aeton returned, hastily belting a tunic that barely reached mid-thigh. "Clova, what's going on?"

"He barged in."

"He didn't knock?"

"No," said Hercules, "he didn't." He grabbed the necklace back, ignored the woman's huff of protest, and spotted two large chests set against the far wall. Three strides took him over, one hand flipped up a lid, and the other snapped out to stop Aeton when he made a move to interfere.

"I don't like you," Hercules said as he reached in for the clothes neatly folded inside. "I don't like you two at all," he added as he tossed the clothes onto the floor.

"Aeton, stop him!" Clova snapped.

"I say," Aeton said without moving. "I say, this isn't right. We'll have you fired, you know."

"Hell, we'll have him hanged," Clova snarled as she jumped to her feet.

Aeton smiled tolerantly. "Now, Clova." He walked over to Hercules and peered into the chest. "She gets that way sometimes, you know. Pre-performance jitters." He looked up at him slyly. "What's your excuse?"

Hercules looked back at him, looked into the now empty chest, and shifted to the second one.

"Oh," Aeton said nervously. "Say, I really don't think—"

"Aeton, will you please stop him?" Clova demanded, red-faced.

More clothes, a few leather belts and straps, a heavily studded wrist band, amazingly heeled boots, and . . .

"Aha," he said.

"Oh," said Aeton.

Clova only growled.

Hercules closed the chest and sat on it, the necklace dangling from his hand. "You hired four men to work with you. They created diversions in each town you went to, while you—the both of you—made nightly visits to the richest houses. Not too difficult with your . . . talents." He held up the necklace. "Does this belong to Olivia Stellas?"

Aeton said nothing; Clova glared.

"I had a meeting with those four men, by the way." He tossed the necklace to Clova, who grabbed it one-handed and clutched it against her chest.

"They've left town. Permanently. You two, on the other hand, will probably find yourselves new places to stay. Like a cell, for instance."

"Kill him," Clova said flatly. "Kill him."

Aeton scratched the top of his head. "Alone?"

"Hell, no, I'll help you."

"Well," he said, looking apologetically at Hercules. "That's all right, then." And he pulled an astonishingly long dagger from the back of his tunic. "Just be careful of the blood, dear. It's too late to wash again."

Hercules hadn't really expected them to put up much of a fight, but it wasn't long before he had the sinking feeling that being caught in a whirlwind was something like this.

Aeton feinted with the dagger, causing Hercules to jump back onto the chest, and because the ceiling wasn't very high, he was forced into an awkward half-crouch.

Then Clova tossed the mirror to Aeton, who sidearmed it at Hercules, who jumped onto the other chest just before Aeton stabbed with the dagger, forcing him to jump back and nearly lose his balance. Which was when Clova sidearmed a candlestick, forcing him to leap onto the first chest again.

Aeton stabbed.

Hercules jumped.

Clova disappeared into the other room.

"It isn't going to work," Hercules said, bracing himself to leap at Aeton.

"Sure it will."

Clova returned, juggling a number of clubs at such a speed that he couldn't count how many there were.

They also, he noted, had little spikes around their tips.

Suddenly one flew from the pack into Aeton's waiting hand, and he instantly spun it at Hercules' head.

Hercules ducked, jumped to avoid a second one, a third, tried to jump up to avoid the one aimed at his feet, hit the ceiling, saw stars, and slipped off the lid to the floor. He landed on his hands and knees and scuttled sideways, but not quickly enough to avoid being struck on the left shoulder.

The spikes weren't long, but they hurt like hell.

"Nice," Clova said, adding the dagger and a chair to the remaining clubs in the air.

"I try," Aeton replied modestly.

Hercules crouched against the wall, realizing that watching Clova was wrong—he needed to watch her husband, watch for the hand that twitched just before she sent him another weapon. "You won't get away," he said.

Aeton grinned. "He's trying to distract us, dear."

"Now, Aeton, you know that means he thinks he's smart."

Another club, which slammed into the wall over Hercules' head and stuck there.

He reached up for it, and snatched his hand down when another club tried to sever it at the wrist.

Next time, Hercules thought; it has to be the next time. If Aeton gets the dagger next . . .

It was the chair.

Hercules stood, caught it with both hands, turned, and used its momentum to fling it as hard as he could at Aeton.

Aeton deftly backflipped out of the way, but the move gave Hercules the chance to grab the empty chest and slide it across the floor after him. Aeton landed, the chest caught him across the shins, and he toppled over it, rolled, came up grinning, and gawked when Hercules grabbed him around the waist.

"I say," the man said.

"Aeton," Clova cried.

"My turn," Hercules told her, and tossed her her husband.

The amazing thing was, for a split second she actually seemed torn between catching him, dodging him, or shielding herself with him while she used the dagger, the only weapon left in her hand.

The hesitation cost her.

Aeton sailed over her right shoulder and met the wall with his skull. When her eyes flicked over to see if he was all right, Hercules threw himself at her legs, tackled her, and pinned her arms to the floor.

"I'll kill you," she spat.

Aeton moaned.

She wriggled, twisted, and said, "You can't kill a woman, Hercules. I know you too well."

Surprised that she knew him at all, he admitted that it would take an immensely dire situation before he would even begin to consider killing a woman.

Clocking her a good one on the jaw, on the other hand, was not beyond the realm of possibility, especially when the husband was beginning to stir, and the wife was trying to toss him the dagger.

He clocked her.

Her eyes closed.

He clocked Aeton, just to be sure, and because the twerp deserved it, and rocked back onto his heels just as Flovi stepped into the room.

"By the gods!" he exclaimed. mustache all a-quiver. "What's going on here?"

Hercules wiped a sheen of sweat from his brow, and winced at the sharp pain in his upper arm. "You'd better tell Salmoneus he's going to need a new act tonight."

"Hercules, you're bleeding."

He was, but not badly. With Flovi's help, he bound the spike holes in his arm with a length of clean cloth; then, as he explained what had happened, he tore a cloak into strips which they used to bind the thieves.

"Amazing," Flovi said, shaking his head in wonder. "We owe you a lot, Hercules. It's over now, right?"

"Oh, no," he answered softly, glancing out the window. "No, Flovi, I'm afraid it's just beginning."

# 15

Dragar stood by his window, staring contemptuously down at the street, at the pedestrians scurrying by, at those still straightening up from the "shift" the night before.

He was angry, and he was excited—or as excited as he ever permitted himself to get.

Angry, because Aulma hadn't returned to the room since last night. Although she was completely extraneous to his plan, he had grown used to having her around. He had even considered blessing her with continued life so that she might remain with him when he introduced to these peasants the terrors and benefits of his new world.

That the gods might intervene didn't worry him.

He had long ago decided that they didn't much care what he did as long as he didn't bother them.

Or threaten them.

That was one mistake he definitely did not plan to make.

Aulma was another. He had allowed her beauty to distract him, and that wouldn't do.

She hadn't returned when she was supposed to, and so, quite simply, she would have to die.

That was part of his excitement—for tonight he would take the first major step in the creation of his world, the establishment of his rule. He hadn't believed it would happen so soon, and he certainly hadn't counted on having so little opposition. But these fools had accepted his tricks and stunts as nothing more than magic; diversions and sleights-of-hand to brighten their drab little lives.

The only thing standing in his way now, as far as he could reckon, was that strongman the idiot Salmoneus had brought into the troupe.

He didn't know why the man was a potential hurdle; he only sensed it. Certainly the man wouldn't be able to stop the forces Dragar could release; he most certainly wouldn't be able to avoid a swift journey to meet Hades.

Nevertheless, Dragar had learned the hard way to trust the growing power of that sense which, he had discovered, normal people didn't have. It told him the man was a possible threat, and that was all he needed to know.

The spell he had woven during their first meeting would keep the threat at a safe distance; the next spell would take care of it permanently.

He smiled to himself, reached out, and grabbed the staff.

His left hand stroked the ram's silver head as one would caress the head of a lover.

His fingers traced the curves of the golden horns, the planes of the jaw, the outline of the skull.

When the fingers stopped, all sound and motion ceased to be.

Then the ram's left eye opened.

And the room filled with green fire.

The arena was nearly empty.

Salmoneus stood in the center, practicing a new introduction, while a handful of musicians sat against the wall and listened in attitudes varying from bored to sleeping. Virgil and Aulma stood well off to one side, looking desperately as if they wanted to hold hands but didn't dare.

When Hercules and Flovi arrived, Flovi immediately joined his fellow band members, while Hercules, after a couple of false starts, told Salmoneus about Clova and Aeton, adding that the duo were already in the hands of the town's proper authorities.

The first thing Salmoneus did was embrace him with rib-straining gratitude, praising him for finally lifting the jinx that had plagued his troupe; the second thing he did was vow at the top of his voice to make a pilgrimage to all the towns the troupe had visited, so he could personally return all the stolen items to their owners; the third thing was, before he could be stopped, to hug Hercules a second time for the idea of giving a show to help the people of Phyphe regain their good spirits.

"Brilliant!" he cried as Hercules eased him back with a pained smile. "I should have thought of that myself."

For a second, then, he seemed to have lost his voice. His face paled, his hands began to tremble, and Hercules searched the arena for signs of impending disaster. There was none; at least none that he could see.

"Oh, no!" Salmoneus wailed. "What am I going to do about a new act at this late date?" He threw up his hands. "I'm ruined. I'm going to be poverty-stricken! I'm going to—"

"Use Flovi," Hercules suggested without thinking.

"What?"

Hercules nodded toward the musician. "He's been wanting to sing for an audience, right? Well, now's his chance."

Salmoneus moved closer and lowered his voice. "Hercules, this is no joke here."

"I'm not joking."

"You have to be joking, you've heard him sing. Or whatever that is."

Hercules had to concede the point. Still, he couldn't resist the urge not only to help Flovi, but also to watch Salmoneus squirm. "Don't worry. Once he gets in front of an audience, he'll be fine. All he needs is a chance to prove himself."

"Ruin me, you mean," Salmoneus grumbled.

"Ruin who?" Flovi wanted to know, ambling over with a flute in his hand.

"Ruin the surprise," Hercules answered quickly.

"What surprise?"

"That you're going to sing tonight."

**139**

"What?" Flovi tried to smile. "Me? Here? Tonight? Sing? A song? Me?"

"Maybe," Salmoneus said, "this is a little sudden."

"Sudden? This? Me?"

"Salmoneus," Hercules warned.

"Sing?" Flovi said, staring at his flute.

"I'm just trying to be sensitive to the needs of the artist," Salmoneus protested.

"In that case, be sensitive to me," Hercules said, cocking a *watch it* eyebrow.

"Tonight?" Flovi whispered. "Me? Sing?"

"Oh, boy." Salmoneus rubbed his hands over his eyes. "We're ruined."

"Ruined?" Flovi grinned. "Sing? Me?" The grin faded. "All by myself alone with no one else just me alone?"

"Swell," Salmoneus muttered. "He's going to faint."

Flovi wandered away, the flute forgotten in his hand.

"Ruined," Salmoneus moaned. "Ruined." Hercules didn't think it would be that bad. If Flovi was able to keep the melody well in sight, maybe the audience would forgive a clunker now and then. Still, he made it clear with a look that the showman owed him a favor; Salmoneus, with a look of his own, made it clear that he would do it, but only under extreme duress and, probably, as long as he and the proceeds had a head start to the next country.

"You worry too much," Hercules told him with a smile, and looked over the man's head when he

**140**

saw Virgil and Aulma inching toward him.

"Sir?" Virgil said nervously. "Sir, may we have a word?"

Hercules had no idea what they wanted, and was about to join them when Salmoneus said, "Oh, gods . . . ," and took a step back, lips quivering in a vain attempt to form new words.

Slowly Hercules turned to the south tunnel.

Oh, boy, he thought.

Peyra entered the arena, her eyes puffed and red, her stride uncertain.

Behind her was Agatra.

Aulma squealed softly and instantly threw her arms around Virgil's waist; Virgil gulped loudly and threw his arms around Aulma's shoulders; the band muttered but didn't move; Flovi didn't know what to do or say and so did and said nothing.

The Harpy was angry.

Her powerful talons clicked loudly on the arena's cobblestone floor, her wings were half-spread to add size to her bulk, and her arms were folded tightly across her feathered chest.

No one made a sound.

When she reached Hercules, she glared and said, "What have you done?"

"Nothing, yet," he admitted.

"You felt it?" she demanded, her harsh voice echoing off the empty rows of seats.

He nodded. So, involuntarily, did the others.

"Then what are you waiting for?"

"One thing at a time, Agatra," he said calmly. "I had something else to do first."

The Harpy huffed, and snapped her fingers. Peyra moved to stand beside her. "Show him," Agatra commanded.

Peyra wasn't quite successful in swallowing a sob, and Hercules didn't like the cold feeling that settled in his stomach.

"What is it?" he asked her gently.

She reached into her pouch and pulled out the yellow frog. "He's . . ." A tear slithered down her cheek.

Salmoneus snickered when he saw the amphibian, but whatever he was going to say was silenced by the look Hercules gave him.

Peyra took a deep shuddering breath. "He's dying."

The frog, unlike previous times, didn't automatically flip onto its back. It lay on her palm with closed eyes, and when Hercules leaned closer for a better look, he could see that it was barely breathing.

"He won't eat," Peyra said, wiping her eyes with the back of her free hand. "He can't eat people food, and I guess, because he's still partly human, he won't eat what he should because of the way he is." A tender finger stroked the frog's head; it didn't stir. "I think he's giving up."

By this time curiosity had overcome the others' fear of the Harpy, and they gathered close, to stare at the frog as much as at Agatra.

"Boy, that sucker is ugly," Salmoneus blurted. Then pointed quickly. "The frog, I mean."

"He may be ugly to you," Peyra sobbed, "but he's my husband, and I love him!"

"Your husband?" Flovi said.

"It's a long story," Hercules answered.

"It'd have to be."

Salmoneus leaned closer. "Does he dance?"

Hercules slapped his shoulder hard, knocking him sideways.

"We danced at our wedding," Peyra wailed.

Salmoneus looked at Flovi. "I'd pay to see that."

Hercules raised his hand again, and Salmoneus ducked behind the musician, his expression bewildered. "What'd I say?"

Then Agatra gestured sharply, and Peyra, tears drenching her cheeks, returned the frog to her pouch.

"He'll be dead by tomorrow," the Harpy said. "If you won't do something before then, I will."

Salmoneus finally saw the light—and the way the Harpy looked at him—and nudged Hercules' arm. "Are you saying this was . . . Dragar?"

"Of course, Dragar, you chubby little chit," Agatra snapped. "Who else do you think did this?"

Insulted, Salmoneus drew himself up. "Madam, or whatever, Dragar is a solid, upstanding member of my esteemed . . . He certainly hasn't the . . ." He looked up at Hercules. "By the gods," he whispered. "Last night. All the other times. But he's—"

"I know, I know," Hercules said. "Just a magician." He shook his head. "No, he's not, Salmoneus. He's much more than that now."

"Then why didn't you do something?" Salmoneus demanded, outraged and righteous. "This poor woman is distraught beyond words!"

Oh, Hercules thought, you're good, boy, you're really good.

"An enchantment," he replied, more to Agatra than his friend. "It must have been on that first day, when we met. Whatever he did, it scattered my thinking, delayed me. I . . ." He frowned at the sky. The overcast had thickened in places, the bulges of growing clouds ominously dark amid the gray. "I didn't realize it until last night."

"Then why do you know it now?" Virgil asked innocently.

Agatra laughed, but the laugh held no humor. "Because he is who he is, that's why. It didn't last."

The young man and Aulma exchanged puzzled glances. "But who is he?"

"Oh," Salmoneus said with an offhanded gesture, "he's just Hercules. It must be a demigod thing."

Virgil gaped; Aulma gaped; they gaped at each other before gaping in tandem at him.

"In that case, sir," Virgil said at last, "I really think you'd better hear what Aulma has to say."

"Not if she's going to slug me," Hercules told him, and held up a hand to forestall any questions. By the faint blush on Aulma's cheeks, he didn't think this was the time to explain about swimming naked in the pool.

Flovi grinned then and pointed. "Company," he said.

Now what? Hercules wondered, and turned to see a large white duck waddle out of the north tunnel, the same duck that had fallen from Dragar's sleeve that first afternoon. It muttered to itself as it wandered across the floor, then froze when it spotted Agatra.

Agatra scowled.

The duck waddled over as fast as it could, looked up at the Harpy, uttered a long quacking sigh, rolled its eyes, and keeled over.

They stared at the unconscious bird for several seconds, until Flovi said, "I think it's in love."

Agatra transferred her glare from the duck to the musician, who shrugged, looked over his shoulder, pointed again, and said again, "Company."

This time, however, there was no amusement in his voice.

# 16

Growling out of the north tunnel was the shaggy, black-and-white dog Hercules had seen rooting around the streets, the one who wouldn't accept the offered food. At first, he didn't see what had caused Flovi's reaction, not until the dog stepped fully out of the tunnel's shadow.

It was half again as large as it had been, its fangs extending below its lower jaw. A pair of horns pointed forward from behind its pointed ears, and several spikes poked out of the thick fur along its spine.

Its eyes flared green.

As soon as the others realized it wasn't interested in them, they bolted for the nearest wall to scramble up, with help or alone, into the front row. Agatra grabbed Peyra and used her wings to lift them to safety. Flovi grabbed the duck.

Hercules didn't move.

He had seen monsters before, some hideous beyond description, but this . . . this *thing* . . . was

**146**

worse, because it had once been normal, nothing more than a scavenger that lived in an alley's shadows.

Magic had somehow given way to sorcery.

Gaze steady, a rasping growl in its throat, the dog lowered its head slightly and moved toward him, one slow step at a time, not once shifting its eyes from Hercules' throat.

Its tail didn't twitch.

When it was ten feet away, it stopped, and he could see the slanted eyes more clearly, the deadly glint of its fangs, and the bubbles of dark froth that began to drip from its mouth.

"A sword, a bow," he heard Salmoneus say. "Doesn't anyone carry a weapon around here?"

There was no answer.

The spellbound animal shifted its haunches, growling louder. Deeper.

Hercules braced himself, even as he felt twinges of stiffness in his left shoulder. A fitful breeze slipped out of the tunnel; the clear noxious scent of burning sulfur wrinkled his nose, and his eyes threatened to water.

The dog lifted its muzzle and sniffed the air, the froth now dripping heavily, in strands.

Hercules glanced at his arm. The wounds he'd received from Aeton and Clova had reopened. And the thing smelled his blood.

That split second was all the animal needed—it gathered its haunches and, as Salmoneus cried a warning, it leapt for Hercules' throat.

Instinctively Hercules threw up his right arm to

block the charge. The dog's jaws clamped harmlessly around the arm guard, but its weight bore them both to the ground. Hercules landed on his back, grunting when his head struck the cobbles. As the animal's rear paws tried to claw a hole through his stomach, he snapped his arm out, slamming the dog sideways to the ground.

Still, it wouldn't let go. Its paws scrabbled frantically against the cobblestones, trying to find purchase so it could stand and charge again.

As it struggled, Hercules got to his knees, and before the creature could shift its grip from the guard to his flesh, he whirled and snapped the arm out again.

The jaws released their hold, and the dog flew howling across the arena and into the wall.

Where it exploded into blinding sparks that spiraled into the cloudy sky.

Salmoneus stood in front of him, hands shaking, his face mottled with indignation. "That . . . that thing! Do you realize it wasn't real?" As if the creature were a personal affront.

Hercules took several deep breaths to clear his nostrils of the stench of sulfur. "So I noticed."

"It could have killed us!"

"In the first place, it was after me, not you," Hercules reminded him as he rose unsteadily to his feet. "In the second place, I don't think it was a serious attack."

"You could have fooled me," Flovi said, coming up behind him with Virgil and Aulma.

"It was a warning, that's all. If I had died, that would have been a bonus."

Salmoneus looked up at them all, panicked. "A warning?" he squeaked. "Just a warning?" He grabbed Hercules' legs and used them to haul himself to his feet. "Just a warning? About what? Is he trying to stop my show?"

"I think," Hercules said, "he has more important things on his mind, Salmoneus. No offense."

Salmoneus sputtered his renewed indignation, raised a fist to make a point, and yanked it down when a shadow passed over them and a hard wind made them squint.

Agatra hovered overhead, wings flapping slowly. "If you don't take care of it," she said to Hercules, "I will." And she flew off toward the woods.

"Why is she so mad at you?" Flovi asked, keeping his voice down.

"She protects her own," Hercules explained. "Peyra's village is her family now. And trust me, Flovi, no one messes with a Harpy's family."

They saw Peyra, alone in the seats, huddled against herself, staring at her knees. Even at this distance he could see the glimmer of tears on her face.

Puzzled, the musician scratched through his hair. "But if Dragar can do . . . you know . . . she'll be killed."

"Yes. She will."

Flovi looked at him with a half smile. "You always get yourself into things like this?"

Hercules shrugged. "Only with Salmoneus."

"Hey," Salmoneus protested. "While you two

are worried about a giant chicken—not to mention slandering my good name—you may have forgotten we were nearly dead here.''

Hercules held up a hand for silence, then walked away slowly, glancing once at the sky, once at the spot where he had flung the unnatural dog. He put his hands on his hips and half-closed his eyes; he rolled a pebble absently beneath his boot; he sniffed, he wiped his face, he turned back to the others and wished they wouldn't look at him like that.

As if he knew all there was to know, and could solve all their problems with a snap of his fingers.

They were frightened.

They had a right to be.

He wasn't doing all that well himself, if he wanted to be honest; which he really didn't. The kind of power Dragar had shown them was nearly godlike in its scope. No man had a right to such knowledge, not to use it the way he feared Dragar would.

He gave them an *I'm on the job* smile.

They gave him grimaces that made him wince.

Suddenly he snapped his fingers, they jumped, and he beckoned to Aulma. She hesitated, grabbed Virgil's arm, and dragged him over with her.

"Dragar," he said, "still doesn't know who I am, does he?"

"No, I'm pretty sure he doesn't."

"So he probably thinks that spell is still working."

She poked a strand of hair from her eyes and allowed him a small smile. "I guess you're right. He . . . he acts the way he does—like he's not paying

150

attention all the time—so people won't know what he's really like." She hugged herself and stood closer to Virgil. "He's cold, Hercules. Like winter sometimes. And he refuses to admit when he makes a mistake. As far as he's concerned, he doesn't make them. Period."

And a more dangerous man for it, Hercules thought.

"All right, then. Now all I need is a reason. I need to know what he's up to."

"My dinars," Salmoneus gasped in alarm, clutching his purse tightly.

"I doubt it, my friend. With what he seems to be able to do, I don't think money is of much use to him at all."

Virgil cleared his throat. "I think that's why you should listen to Aulma, sir. I think she knows."

Just after Dragar took her on as an assistant, Aulma told them, he came back from a walk in the wood carrying a large scroll. He refused to allow her to see it, even though he knew she couldn't read. That didn't bother her, not really; she was used to people treating her that way, and he was, otherwise, very kind to her.

The next day he insisted they go to Sparta, where he spent the better part of a week visiting various silver- and goldsmiths. By the time he was done, the ram's head had been created. That, too, he refused to allow her to touch.

That night there was a fire in his room, and when she ran in to see what had happened, he was standing amid a pile of ashes. He claimed he had accidentally set the scroll afire while testing a new trick, but she didn't believe him. He might act strange, but he was never careless.

He was never the same again.

He grew more distant, more suspicious of other people, and more anxious about his act. As soon as he heard about Salmoneus, he rushed to join the troupe, even though he admitted they would probably make more money on their own.

The first night, in a place called Brethan, he passed out in the middle of the town square. She thought he had died. When he recovered an hour later, he was more excited than she'd ever seen him. It happened again in Immanus. And again in Hyanth.

He called it a "tingling."

She hadn't felt a thing.

But each time it happened, he had the ram's head with him; and after each incident, he would lock himself in his room for hours, refusing all food and water, all attempts at communication. She heard muttering and chanting, nothing more.

She saw an eerie green glow beneath the door.

And after each of these strange session, something strange would happen.

Each time more frightening than the last.

"He . . ." Aulma clasped her hands at her mouth and shook her head. "After that first time in Brethan, he didn't talk to me for two days. Then he started saying weird things, like, would I like to have as many slaves as I want, and wouldn't it be fun to watch this village or that disappear into the ground.

"He scared me so much, I didn't dare run away. I wanted to, but I couldn't. Besides, in the beginning, I thought he was kidding.

"Then he came here, to this arena. Alone. When he came out, he looked as if he had seen a ghost, and he told me that it was all over. He had it all, and now he was ready."

With a trembling finger she pointed at the thickening clouds. "He did that. He made the ground move. He turned that poor man into that frog. A test, he called it. A game.

"He wants to be in charge, Hercules. He wants everyone to bow to him. And if you won't be his slave, he'll kill you.

"He doesn't care which you choose. That's the really frightening part—he doesn't care which."

Hercules watched helplessly as Aulma burst into silent tears, turning to Virgil for the comfort of his arms. Virgil, for his part, looked too terrified to breathe.

Salmoneus took a step toward the nearest exit, and changed his mind; he pointed at Flovi, opened his mouth to say something, and changed his mind; he took another step toward the exit, gave everyone a wan smile, took another step, threw up his hands and sighed.

"We can't go, can we?" he said to Hercules.

"I wish we could."

"He's a kind of sorcerer now, isn't he?"

Hercules nodded solemnly.

"He's going to fry us, right?"

"Not if I can help it."

"But what can you do?" Flovi asked. "You saw what he did to that poor dog."

"We could pray to the gods," Virgil suggested.

Hercules looked over to Peyra, still weeping in her seat. "No, that might take too long. Besides, they might not be in the mood."

Salmoneus looked around in a panic. "Well, we can't just go on, business as usual."

Suddenly Hercules grinned. "You know... maybe we can."

They followed his gaze to Peyra, who was no longer alone. The duck had regained consciousness, and had waddled over to her, laying its head in her lap. She stroked its back gently, and for the first time that day she actually smiled.

"I don't get it," Salmoneus said.

Hercules tapped his temple with a finger. "I'm not sure I do either, my friend, but this is what you're going to do."

"Run?" Salmoneus asked hopefully.

"The show."

"You're kidding."

"This place is where it begins," Hercules reminded him. "The beginning of whatever Dragar has in mind. Conquering the world, enslaving us all, whatever sickness has taken him." He jabbed a finger at the man's chest. "You are going to put on the best show you've ever done. You're going to make this a night to remember."

"He conquers the world, I'll remember that pretty good, too," Salmoneus grumbled.

Hercules laughed. "A long show, Salmoneus. I'm going to need time."

"For what?"

"Do you really want to know?"

Salmoneus almost said yes, but changed his mind and shook his head.

Flovi tugged at his mustache. "And here I thought I'd be able to find out what the mystery of this place is for me, for my destiny."

"You will," Hercules assured him.

"So will I still be alive to enjoy it?"

"Sure," Hercules promised, and pulled Salmoneus to one side. He gave three instructions: that the show be big, noisy, and above all, long; that Dragar, no matter what, be the last act; and, more importantly, that nothing happen to Peyra until he returned.

"I'm counting on you," he said gravely. "Don't screw it up."

Surprisingly Salmoneus didn't look hurt. "For a change?"

"I didn't say that."

"You were thinking it."

"It was tempting."

Salmoneus smiled and shook his head before his expression grew somber. "I won't screw it up, Hercules. By the all the gods, I swear it."

Hercules nodded. And grinned. "Sure you will."

Salmoneus didn't know whether to laugh or throw a punch, and so said, "For gods' sake, then, please get back before Flovi sings, or I'm ruined."

"I will," Hercules answered, and prayed it wouldn't prove to be a lie.

# 17

Dragar wasn't in his room, and no one at the inn knew where he had gone.

Not that Hercules had expected anything else. That would have been too easy: sitting down with the man, making sure the conquering and enslaving was what he had in mind, and then doing something about it.

He walked slowly along the narrow street, side-stepping carts and horses, watching repairs being made, listening to people talk about the "shift" the night before, and about the big show at the arena. Apparently Virgil and his help had already begun to make their way through town, announcing the special performances, at special prices, with extra special appearances by extra special people.

Hercules had a feeling the place would be packed.

A stop at a fruit vendor's stall told him Dragar had passed by only a few minutes before, muttering to himself and paying no attention to the bustle around him.

Another stop, this time at a blacksmith's, made it clear the magician was on his way out of town.

Hercules had to force himself not to run. Which he probably couldn't have done even if he wanted to, which he did, since he was stopped every few yards by someone who recognized the Red Power Beast and wanted to know if he could really bend iron bars with his ears.

Virgil, it appeared, was laying it on a little thick.

By the time he arrived at Phyphe's north exit, too much time had passed. Dragar was long gone. The road, while not crowded, was busy, as travelers rode and walked into town; by the bits of conversation he overheard, he deduced that most of them were here to do some business, then attend the show.

"Packed," he decided, was undoubtedly an understatement.

He walked on, keeping to the verge as Phyphe slipped away behind him, doing his best not to give in to anxiety, or the unpleasant feeling that he was headed in the wrong direction.

Here was mostly open land that rolled gently to the horizon. Mostly farms, he reckoned, and probably a few scattered estates of the area's most wealthy families. A few lonely trees. A creek.

But still no sign of Dragar.

Frustration made him impatient. He walked, ran a few steps, walked again, and glared at the sky, where the overcast had finally coalesced into thick clouds streaked with white and gray. A slow, damp wind pushed through the high grass. A flock of crows circled in the distance.

Crazy, he thought; this is crazy. If I keep this up, I'll end up in Sparta.

Maybe he would have to wait until tonight after all.

With a grunt of disgust he turned around, and grunted again when he saw it: several hundred yards away on his right, across an unused field, was an arm of the forest that marched to Phyphe from the south. He had been so intent on following the road that he hadn't noticed it before, almost indistinguishable from the gloom where the land met the horizon.

Without hesitation he ran into the long grass, pacing himself and hoping he wasn't making a mistake.

If he was, he would never get back in time.


Virgil slumped against the wall of a shop that sold jars and plates and decorative copper shields.

He was exhausted, and his vision had grown a little blurry.

He and the local band had split up as soon as Hercules left the arena, each of them instructed to spread the word of the benefit performance to as many people as they could. With Aulma unwilling to leave his side, he decided that the taverns and inns were good places to start, because the news would spread more quickly there, but he hadn't counted on how many inns and taverns there were in a little place like this.

But at least he hadn't run into Olivia.

That would have killed him.

And if that didn't kill him, Aulma would, before Olivia could.

Wouldn't you know it, he thought as he panted; a guy goes for years without a single woman paying any attention to him, then suddenly there are two.

He leaned over, hands braced on his knees, and waited for his lungs to catch up.

He wasn't sure exactly what was going on, even with all that weird stuff Aulma had told them, but he had a strong feeling it was worse than his admittedly feeble imagination could manage.

"Aulma," he said, swallowing hard, "when this is over, do you think you could stand leaving show business?" ·

He laughed shortly. Now that was a particularly stupid question considering what Dragar had gone to her.

"So what do you think?"

She didn't answer.

He took one more deep breath and straightened, rested his hands on his hips, and grinned sheepishly. "I don't want you to get the wrong idea, though. I mean, I'm not really asking you to do anything—"

"You drunk?"

That wasn't Aulma.

He blinked, turned his head, and saw a tall man in a plain robe staring at him oddly. "No, I am not drunk."

The shopkeeper scratched through his skimpy beard. "Then who are you talking to?"

Virgil pointed. "Aulma."

"Aulma who?"

Virgil looked.

Aulma was gone.

"Aulma?" He stepped into the crowded street. "Aulma?"

"Drunk," the shopkeeper muttered and returned inside.

Virgil forgot about the announcements; he had to find the woman he was pretty sure he was in love with before something happened to her.

"Aulma!" he called. "Aulma!"

Salmoneus paced back and forth outside the arena.

Although he had every confidence in Hercules, he still couldn't help feeling that vaudalville was dead. Even if Dragar was defeated ... even *when* Dragar was defeated, word would spread, no town or village would risk the vaudalvillian jinx, and he'd be left with a dozen chests of clothes he wouldn't be caught dead in. Except maybe the purple thing with the gold trim and the glittery stuff on the hem.

His fingers brushed across his paunch. His stomach growled, demanding food, but he didn't dare eat because he didn't think his nerves would let him keep it all down.

A footstep made him jump.

"Sorry," Peyra whispered.

"It's all right." He smiled with more confidence than he felt. "I'm just rehearsing." He tapped his temple. "In here."

At her side the large white duck quacked softly.

"No," Salmoneus said. "I do not know where the Harpy is."

The duck sighed and wandered away.

Peyra gasped. "You speak duck?"

Salmoneus gave her a look. "Lucky guess."

Tenderly she lifted her husband from his pouch and stroked his back with one finger. The frog didn't move. "I know how he feels."

Salmoneus looked at the frog, looked at the duck, looked at the sky, and thought, This isn't a jinx, it's a curse, right? You're getting back at me for that air-sandal thing, aren't you?

"Salmoneus?"

"Yes?"

"Are we going to be all right?"

He nodded without hesitation. "Hercules promised. And no matter how it looks, he never goes back on a promise."

She looked at his hands. "Then how come your fingers are crossed?"

"Insurance."

"What's that?"

I don't know, he thought, but it damn well better work.

It was the arena, Hercules thought as he ran across the empty field; it was the overwhelming surge of power that he had felt.

He knew that here and there throughout the many lands he had traveled there were places marked by certain mystical properties. He had no idea why this was so, and none of the gods he knew had ever explained it. Of course, they didn't have to; they were gods.

He had also believed that no human could ever tap this energy, but that was obviously untrue.

Dragar had.

If Aulma was right, the answer must have been in the scroll the man had found. It had told him how to take that power for his own.

The power he had concentrated in the head of the silver ram.

Hercules slowed as he approached the trees, wondering why it was that the good guys never found stuff like that. It would certainly, for example, make his life a whole lot easier, and he wouldn't have to work up such a big sweat taking care of the bad guys.

Bad guys who could enchant demigods, however briefly, were never any fun. Especially for the good guys.

He saw the first sign of passage then, grass that had been trampled recently and was just now beginning to recover. He followed the faint trail until he spotted a narrow path that led deeper into the woodland.

The trees were still widely spaced, their high branches filtering what little light there was into patches of lesser gloom that swayed and shifted as the wind touched the trees.

He flexed his fingers as he moved on, much as a cat will twitch its tail.

Birds called faintly.

A growing tension in the air raised the hairs on the back of his neck.

He scolded himself for not bringing someone with him; preferably an army, perhaps two.

Maybe, he thought, this wasn't such a hot idea.

It was one thing to tangle with Hera. Her motives were perfectly clear: she wanted him dead, and she didn't care what she did to accomplish it. Monsters and assassins were his stepmother's preferred modes of attack; nothing terribly subtle as far as she was concerned.

He kind of missed that now.

Dragar, on the other hand, was human. And humans were far too complicated. They liked intrigue and convoluted plots and manipulations of people who didn't know they were being manipulated; they liked wars that purported to be about one thing but were, in reality, about something else you never even thought of until it was too late.

It was as if they had seen how the gods worked and had decided that was too boring.

Still, there was a lot to be said for boring.

For one thing, it was boring.

He stepped into a wide, deep clearing just as a rent in the clouds allowed afternoon sunlight through.

He saw low weeds and virtually no grass; patches of bare earth that were a sickly pale brown.

"It suits you," he said aloud.

"Thank you," said Dragar, stepping out from behind a tree on the far side. "But you could have found a better place to die, don't you think?"

He wore a long black robe, with a hood edged in

silver that shimmered like fire. In his left hand was the staff.

"Dying," said Hercules, "isn't part of the deal."

"Deal, strongman? What deal?"

"The deal that says I won't hurt you if you destroy that staff."

Dragar laughed, a deep laugh that rolled through the woods like a deep winter's wind.

Hercules shrugged without moving—it was a worth a shot, you never knew when a bad guy might suddenly wake up and repent.

Not that it had ever happened.

But you never knew until you tried.

"Strongman," Dragar said, "you're being a pest. And I have things to do. Please leave me. At once."

Hercules didn't move.

Dragar scowled. "Didn't you hear me? I said leave! At once!"

"I heard you. I'm not going anywhere."

Dragar took a step toward him, his face creased with bewilderment. "But you have to."

"No, I don't."

"Yes, you do."

"Do not."

"Do so."

Hercules sighed. Bad guys were bad enough, but stubborn bad guys were a pain in the ass. "Give it up, Dragar. You're not going to win."

Dragar stared at the ram's head, shook the staff, stared at Hercules, and said, "You're supposed to do what I say, plus have a strong feeling that everything's going to work out in the end without you having to do a thing about it.''

Hercules nodded. "I know."

"Then leave!"

"Nope."

He started across the clearing. Startled, Dragar backed up, his free hand tugging nervously at his goatee. "Do you have a name, strongman?"

"You're the magician, you figure it out."

Dragar lifted the staff over his head. "No time for games."

Hercules smiled. "Exactly." He kept moving. "And it's Hercules, if you have to know."

Dragar froze.

Hercules smiled; at last something was going his way.

Dragar smiled in turn, but it wasn't the smile of a man ready to yield.

Damn, Hercules thought.

"Hercules," Dragar said with a small shake of his head. "How terribly . . . fitting."

That made Hercules pause. "What do you mean?"

Dragar cocked an eyebrow. "That the first man to see the real power of the Eye will be a demigod."

"Meaning what?"

The smile vanished. "Meaning, Hercules, that demigods aren't immortal."

# 18

Hercules backed up slowly, hands out to show that he carried no weapons.

Not that Dragar cared, or was willing to be sporting about it. He lowered the staff and held it in both hands, making sure that Hercules could see the silver face.

So he could see the right eye open.

A silent voice told him that what he saw was impossible, while another suggested that it certainly was possible, because it wasn't magic, it was sorcery, and a third voice didn't give a fig about the difference because they were going to be sizzled if the big guy didn't move.

"Behold the power of the Eye!" Dragar thundered.

A thin beam of pulsing red light flared from the Eye and drew itself into a floating coil as if it were a serpent. Every few seconds sparks flashed to the ground, where they raised tiny puffs of white smoke. The end of the beam flattened and spread, and Hercules swore he could see fangs in there, and the deadened eyes of a cobra.

At the edge of the clearing he tensed to run, his left hand braced against a thick-boled tree. Then he shook his head quickly, because he knew he wouldn't get two steps before that beam-snake struck him.

"Wise, strongman, wise," Dragar said, as though reading his mind. "Better to die facing your enemy than in running away like a coward."

"I don't plan on dying, Dragar."

"Which of us really does?" Dragar set the butt of the staff on the ground by his right foot, but in such a deliberate way that Hercules guessed the beam's connection to the Ram was tenuous at best. "But in the scheme of things, it's inevitable, don't you agree?"

Hercules had no time to respond.

Dragar jerked his arm, and the red beam struck, snapping across the distance between them like the strike of a real snake.

Hercules sprang behind the tree and turned to watch the beam-snake flare against a stubby bush. There was no sound, just a blinding red flash that made him raise an arm to protect his eyes. The light faded instantly, and there was nothing left but a column of smoke, and ash where the bush had been.

"Oh, Hercules," Dragar called, "do you really think that tree will protect you?"

The clearing glowed, and Hercules leapt again to his left, hitting the ground and somersaulting to his feet, then half-turning away as the large tree exploded silently halfway up and he was showered with glowing embers.

This, he thought as he slapped the embers from his hair and clothing, is going to be a problem.

Smoke caught by the wind billowed through the clearing, momentarily obscuring his position. He used the time to grab a rock from the ground and leap again to his left as a green snake struck the ground some five feet away.

"Did I get you, strongman?"

Hercules didn't answer.

"Very wise," Dragar said mockingly. "Or lucky, I suppose."

The smoke cleared.

Dragar spotted him. "Ah. There you are, strongman." He turned the Eye toward him. "Behold!"

"Behold yourself," Hercules said, and threw the rock as hard as he could.

It missed the Ram, but it hit the sorcerer just below the right knee. He cried out and fell, using a desperate grip on the staff to prevent him from falling all the way.

Hercules charged, picking up another, smaller, rock on the run.

Dragar hissed in pain.

Hercules threw the rock without breaking stride, bouncing it off the man's shoulder.

Another painful cry, and Dragar's left arm dangled uselessly at his side.

But the smile returned, and that almost stopped Hercules in the middle of his charge.

"Behold," Dragar whispered, and with one hand

he brought the Ram down to strike the ground.

The earth rippled in a series of impossible waves, their undulation passing under Hercules like the low waves in a bay. But they were enough to throw him off-balance, and he came down hard on one knee, coughing in the thick dust raised by the ripples.

He ignored the brief pain.

Dragar was less than fifteen feet away, still on his knee, only his grip on the staff keeping him from falling. Sweat shone on his face; the muscles of his neck bulged with the effort to keep him upright.

Hercules swayed to his feet.

"Not yet," Dragar said, and struck the ground again.

Hercules thought he was ready, but the ripples spread left and right now, the trees groaning as they rose and fell with the motion, branches creaking, weaker ones snapping off and crashing to the ground.

Which split open at his feet before he realized what had happened.

Desperately he tried to keep one boot on either side of the gap. Below him there was nothing but darkness and roiling dust, and he couldn't hear the stones and rocks hit any kind of bottom when they fell.

Dragar murmured something, and the dust became thick smoke, and in its depths Hercules could see the intermittent glow of fire.

"If you jump," the sorcerer said, his voice taut with pain, "it'll be so much easier."

Hercules was trapped. His legs were so far apart,

he couldn't shift his weight quickly enough to attempt a leap for solid ground. On the other hand, he couldn't stay this way for long either—his legs were also beginning to quiver with the strain of holding him up in this unnatural position. He couldn't bend over, he couldn't straighten, he sure couldn't fly, and where, now that he thought about it, was that damn Harpy when he needed her?

The earth groaned.

The gap widened.

Dragar was on his feet now, leaning heavily on the staff.

"I like this," he said with a nod. "I may use it again."

Heat rose from the chasm; writhing slips of smoke began to coil over the edges.

The fire was brighter.

"They'll find a way, you know," Hercules managed to say, his gaze flicking from the chasm to the sorcerer.

Dragar frowned. "Who? To do what?"

"To kill you."

Dragar laughed silently. "Oh, I don't think so."

Hercules swayed as the gap widened again. "But they will. You can't keep an enchantment on everyone, all the time. You're not that good."

Dragar managed to look down his nose at him without moving his head. "Good enough for a start, Hercules. An army armed with magic doesn't need enchantments all the time."

"You'll never be able to trust anyone."

"So?"

Hercules thought about that one and understood that the man was right: he didn't need to trust anyone, because his magic would do it for him. For those he needed to help run things, there were the spells; for those he didn't need, there was a one-way trip to the Underworld.

If the man wasn't stopped, Hades was going to have his hands full.

A cloud of smoke rose around Hercules, choking him, bringing stinging tears to his eyes.

His left foot slipped, and he began to fall.

Instantly he threw himself in that direction, blindly, striking the uneven chasm wall so hard the air whooshed from his lungs. But his hands caught the ragged lip, gripping it so tightly his fingers threatened to cramp. His legs flailed for a moment before finding tiny rock ledges to push on and slightly relieve the pressure on his arms.

It wasn't perfect, but he was still alive.

All he needed now was a couple of breaths, a couple of seconds, and he could haul himself up and out, no problem.

The earth groaned.

You, he told himself, should keep your big mouth shut.

The gap began to close. In such jerky movement that he nearly lost his grip.

Dragar laughed. "Had enough, strongman?" His voice dropped to a seductive whisper. "Just let go. That's all you have to do. Just let go, and you won't feel a thing."

Hercules closed his eyes and concentrated.

171

"Just let go, strongman. Just let go."

Nothing existed but his hands and arms; all the strength he had was there; nothing else mattered.

"Let go."

He could feel the other side of the gap begin to press against his back.

"Let go."

One chance, and he took it:

He flattened his hands against the ground and pushed as hard and as fast as he could, shooting himself out of the chasm just as an explosion of smoke and fire rose from below and mushroomed into the sky.

The gap slammed shut.

Dragar couldn't believe it.

Hercules walked toward him on legs that barely paid attention to his commands. He was angry, he was hot, his arms burned, and if this half-baked sorcerer thought he was going to set up his own little kingdom and rule the world from it, he had another think coming.

"Oh," Dragar said when he saw Hercules' expression.

Hercules reached out a hand. "Give it to me."

Dragar backed off. "Never!"

"Then use it," he said, daring the magician.

Dragar didn't understand, but he wasn't a complete idiot either. He sneered, the Eye opened, and a flare of orange fire spat from the silver ram.

Hercules jerked up his arm, and the fire shattered harmlessly against the arm guard.

Another flare, blocked just as easily.

Dragar held the staff in both hands and spun it slowly, flinging a rainbow of fiery lances in all directions. Trees exploded, caught fire, split in half, were torn from the ground on roots that were aflame; charred gouges marred the earth; shrubs burned like torches.

The arm guards blocked every attack that reached them.

"You're not human!" Dragar wailed.

Hercules waggled one hand. "Maybe, maybe not." He reached out and yanked the staff from the man's hands. "But you are, my friend, and now your power's mine."

Dragar's eyes opened wide in shock. "You wouldn't dare." The eyes narrowed. "You can't." The eyes widened again. "You don't know how." The eyes narrowed. "You're not the type."

"You're making yourself dizzy," Hercules said.

Dragar passed a hand over his eyes. "I know."

Hercules examined the staff and ram, shook his head, and said, "Let's go. There are some people back in Phyphe who want to talk to you."

Dragar pressed his hands against his chest. "Are you going to hit me?"

"Are you going to come quietly?"

"By the gods, of course not!"

"Then I'm going to have to hit you."

That smile returned, sly and mocking. "Not if I hit you first."

Hercules had to admit, it was kind of admirable that the man didn't know when to quit. It was stupid, too, but Dragar was too dumb to realize it.

"You want to hit me, give it a try."

"Okay." Dragar stood as straight as he could, but he kept his hands at his chest.

Hercules had a bad feeling. Could Dragar do his magic without the ram? He checked the Eye; it was closed.

He checked Dragar, who hadn't moved.

He had a sudden, and thoroughly unpleasant, feeling that he ought to check behind him.

He did.

Aulma belted him with a club, and he went down like a felled tree.

# 19

There were no voices, no whispered concerns for his health, no pleas for him to recover in time to save whatever it was he was supposed to save.

There was, however, a splitting headache.

He groaned, opened his eyes, and stared into the puzzled gaze of a dark brown rabbit, whose twitching nose and exposed sharp teeth suggested an internal debate between the vegetarian it was born to be and the carnivore whose diet wasn't quite as boring and which he maybe ought to give a try.

"Beat it," Hercules muttered.

The rabbit did.

His eyes closed again, and he waited impatiently for the throbbing to subside, and the inner voice to shut up—the one that told him what an idiot he was for thinking a man like Dragar wouldn't have a minion or two lurking about, just in case. Even if the minion, as in Aulma's case, had a glassy stare that suggested a spell had been cast to keep her under control.

Gingerly cradling the back of his head with a palm, he rolled onto his back and stared at the sky.

The clouds had thickened; the light had dimmed.

As he sat up, he braced himself for pain and was pleased that when it came, it wasn't as bad as he had feared. Aulma had hit him a good one, but it had been a glancing blow, most of the force of which had been taken by his shoulder. Which was why, he figured, his shoulder hurt so much.

At least there was no blood.

After some testing and sharp intakes of breath, he made it to his feet, checking his balance along the way. Once he was sure he wouldn't fall, he headed unsteadily for the road, struggling against the urge to run, a sure way to end up on his back again.

At the edge of the woods his head cleared, his limbs had decided to hang around and work for a while, and he figured that maybe this had worked out for the best. Although he doubted Dragar thought him dead, it was entirely possible that the sorcerer believed Hercules was at least out of commission long enough for him to do whatever had to be done to begin his campaign.

It was about the only advantage he had.

It was also one he hadn't the slightest idea how to use.

The plan he had hinted to Salmoneus about dealt with taking care of Dragar before the man had a chance to do anything.

The new plan, which didn't make any more sense than the old one, dealt with taking care of Dragar before he had a chance to do anything. Admittedly the two sounded identical, but he was positive there was a significant, subtle difference, and he was equally positive that he'd recognize it as soon as he saw it.

Long strides took him quickly across the field to the road. It was deserted now, and as he entered Phyphe, so were the streets he passed. Shutters were closed, doors were barred, and he heard nothing but his own breathing, and the thud of his boots on the hard-packed dirt.

He was halfway to the arena before he remembered Agatra's threat: if he didn't do something about Dragar, she would.

But he didn't think she had any idea what the man was really capable of.

Swell, he thought; she'll try to kill him, she'll get her feathers burned off, and with my luck, Hades will stick her with me in the Underworld, and I'll never hear the end of it.

Literally.

A slow wind drifted over the shops and houses. A dust devil darted out of an alley and collapsed at his feet.

The continued silence began to get on his nerves, and he found himself whistling under his breath just to hear some noise.

His right hand twitched.

Every few yards he looked over his shoulder, and saw nothing but twilight shadows slipping out of doorways and down from the eaves.

A broken bench lay in the mouth of an alley. He

tore one of the long, stout legs off, just to have something in his hand.

Imaginary footfalls made him turn and walk backward a few paces.

Whispers from behind closed windows and doors.

A loose section of roof thatch rustling in the wind.

He stopped.

"All right," he said angrily. "That's enough."

Nothing changed, but the sound of his voice shattered the burgeoning apprehension that had settled over him. This was not the same as facing a Cyclops, or a Titan, or an army bent on a helpless village's destruction. But it was a duel nonetheless, between him and an enemy who this time happened to be a sorcerer.

A sorcerer, Hercules realized suddenly, who was in a hurry.

A wisp of a smile crossed his lips.

"Yes," he whispered as he broke into a trot. "Yes, by the gods, yes."

Dragar had power, no question about it. But if Aulma and Salmoneus were right, he had had this power not much more than half a year. And for most of that time, he had been testing it, searching for its limits, determining its control.

But he hadn't mastered it.

If he had, Hercules would have died out there in the woods.

This final locus of energy in the arena, the one that had knocked him senseless, only provided strength to Dragar, not knowledge.

Dragar was a sorcerer, but he still didn't think like

one. He handled his magic like a sword, not like sorcery.

And swords, no matter what they were made of, could still be parried.

He sprinted through the south gate, aware now of the voice of the arena crowd. As he neared the small coliseum, he slowed to a brisk walk. Dozens of torches on high poles affixed to the top of the outer wall held back the gathering darkness, their flames in tight twists and spirals as the wind tried to rip them away. He heard cheers, some laughter, and the very faint sound of carefree music.

No one stood outside.

The performers would be waiting their turns at the north tunnel, Dragar undoubtedly among them.

Hercules went straight to the other entrance, keeping close to the wall. When he reached the gap, he looked around the corner and saw Delilah the Contortionist in the center of the floor. The tunnel itself was empty, and he slipped inside before anyone could spot him.

Thanks to the thatch roofing, there was no light here; until he stepped into the open, he would be invisible.

Switching the bench leg to his left hand, he eased along the wall, stopping at the edge of the torchlight's reach.

As far as he could tell, the arena was packed. The whole town and then some was jammed into the seats, and stood along the back wall on top. Some in the first row leaned so far over that he was sure more than one had already fallen over.

He couldn't see Peyra.

The other tunnel was dark as well. All he could see there was shadows and silhouettes.

Patience, he told himself; there's nothing to do now but wait.

He leaned against the wall and watched Delilah finish her routine. The applause deafened him; flowers were tossed after her as she danced into the exit. From the blossoms already littering the cobblestones, he knew that those who had preceded her had also been well received—as much in relief after the previous night's terror as in appreciation.

He suspected the performers didn't really care.

He grinned at the next act—Olivia Stellas and her declamation, an epic history of Phyphe as written by her own hand. By the amount of parchment she held, Phyphe had been around a really long time.

Then a voice said behind him, "She's really awful, isn't she?"

Hercules wasn't sure which would give out first— his legs or his heart. When neither did, it was a struggle not to wrap his fingers around Salmoneus' throat and throttle him until he turned as red as the garish gown Olivia wore.

Salmoneus lifted his shoulders in a heavy sigh. "I had to let every amateur who can toot on a reed in. Thanks to you."

"What did I do?"

There was no need to whisper—Olivia's voice carried easily, loudly, and shrilly. Had she not been head of the town's ruling council, she probably would have been stoned before she finished the first page. As it was, the crowd quickly realized that lots of cheers and applause would drown most of her out.

There were a lot of cheers and applause.

"You told me to make the show as long as I could," Salmoneus reminded him glumly. He peered at him in the gloom. "You look dreadful, by the way."

"I look worse than I feel."

"Good thing." The chubby showman rubbed his hands together as if trying to keep warm. "Dragar is here. He keeps insisting he has to go on."

"Stall him."

"Why?"

Hercules watched Olivia reach the midway point in her declamation. "I want him as nervous as possible."

"Believe me, Hercules, if he gets more any more nervous, he's going to start shedding."

Hercules laughed and shook his head. It was a good feeling, and he slapped his friend's shoulder in gratitude.

Salmoneus didn't get it, but he returned the smile, albeit a little anxiously. "So what happens now?"

Olivia reached the last page; the walls trembled with the cheers and applause.

"Flovi," Hercules said.

"What?" Salmoneus yelped.

Hercules nodded. "Flovi is next. Let him sing his heart out."

Then, as his friend's eyes widened in disbelief, he explained the rest of his plan.

"What?" Salmoneus yelped.

"Trust me, you'll be famous."

"What?" If Salmoneus' voice had gotten any higher, he would have punctured half the eardrums in the arena.

Hercules clamped his hands on the man's shoulders. "Just do it, Salmoneus. There's no time for explanations."

Salmoneus would have argued, but Olivia was done, the crowd was hysterical with relief, and Hercules shoved him out of the tunnel.

Then he closed his eyes and tried to concentrate.

Listening as Salmoneus introduced Flovi.

Listening as the audience applauded politely.

Listening as Flovi, after several clearings of his throat and a couple of false starts, began "That Old Tavern in the Hills," which was supposed to be a plaintive ballad about a man who lost his love, his cart, and his old dog to a traveling gambling man.

Hercules couldn't help it—he looked.

With the local band doing its best to force Flovi into the melody, Flovi sang his heart out, but not even that mellifluous baritone was able to mask the struggle.

The crowd was silent. Stunned, Hercules figured.

Finally Flovi stopped, lowered his head in abject defeat, and turned to leave.

It was all Hercules could do not to run after him, to console him, to urge him not to give up, not where his dreams were involved.

Suddenly, from the front row on the right, the silence was broken by a single note, the one Flovi couldn't find.

He stopped. He turned. He blinked rapidly in confusion.

The note sounded again.

Hercules eased forward, trying to find out who belonged to that voice, that note.

A woman in a drab brown dress stood, and sang the note again.

It was Merta, the stable girl.

Flovi started the ballad again, and this time Merta joined him. Not a missed note, not a missed beat—what each lacked, the other now provided.

Magic, Hercules thought as he listened; absolute magic.

When they finished, the silence lasted several heartbeats; when it ended, the explosion of adulation was enough to bring tears to the eyes of those whose eyes weren't filled with tears already from the ballad.

Flovi raced to the wall, reached out his arms, and Merta leapt into them. They embraced, they walked back to the center of the arena, and Flovi nodded to a suddenly excited band.

Five more songs. Enough flowers and scarves and coins to bury a small city.

Three encores, more flowers and scarves and coins, and Hercules began to think it would keep up until dawn.

Finally Salmoneus darted out of the other tunnel and, promising that the Fantastic Country Duo would return, hustled them off, then wisely waited until the applause ended before returning.

He stared at the south tunnel, touched his beard, touched his heart.

Hercules took a deep breath; now or never, Salmoneus, don't screw it up.

Salmoneus faced the audience.

"And now, ladies and gentlemen, for your amazement and your astonishment, the Salmoneus Traveling Theater of Fun is proud to present that king of prestidigitation, that monarch of magic, that emperor of—"

He yelped when a small green fireball struck him in the rump.

Then Dragar stepped out of the tunnel, and all the torches went out.

# 20

Hercules felt the audience holding its breath in anticipation, uncertain whether this was part of the act or a prelude to another disaster.

Then Dragar said, "Behold!" And the torches flared again.

He stood in the center of the arena, appearing taller than usual in a dark blue robe fringed and hemmed with braided gold thread. His hair was covered by a silver skullcap, his feet by glittering silver-and-red boots. The darkness of his beard made his face ghostly white; the flicker of the torchlight in his eyes made them glow a pale yellow.

The only thing missing was Aulma and her dancing.

A smattering of tentative applause signaled the audience's continuing misgivings, and even when Dragar smiled, bowed, and plucked blindingly white doves from his voluminous sleeves, to toss lightly into the air, the people still held back.

Hercules could smell it.

It was fear.

Dragar didn't appear to notice. He continued his routine as if nothing were amiss—beautiful doves and gaudy scarves from his sleeves, liquid fire poured like honey from a small jug into a smaller goblet, ribbons from his beard, the now-familiar fireballs that floated over his head and exploded silently into sparks that the wind took into the clouds. The only time he lost the smile was when he walked over to the arena's edge and looked up at a child as if to ask for her assistance, and she cowered against her mother's side.

After a long moment Dragar laughed. "The child knows a charlatan when she sees one," he announced as he returned to the center. "I do believe she has guessed my secrets."

A few people laughed with him, and he acknowledged them with a modest nod.

"But I think," he continued, one hand stroking his goatee, "this will change her mind."

He reached into his robe, frowned as he pretended not to find what he sought, then uttered an "Aha!" as he pulled out the black staff with the head of the silver ram.

This time the applause was a little louder, but it sounded brittle.

Hercules braced himself, wondering if perhaps he had waited too long.

"Behold!" Dragar cried.

"Yes, behold!" Salmoneus cried as he trotted from the other tunnel, waving to the audience and grinning like a madman. "Behold the extra-special attraction we have created just for you, the good and wonderful people of Phyphe.''

Dragar glared at him, too angry to speak, too astonished to move.

"One time only!" Salmoneus announced at the top his near-squeaking voice, ignoring the fuming magician as he trotted awkwardly around the wall, grinning wildly at the faces turned toward him, confused and wondering. "Absolutely guaranteed one time only!"

The crowd began to stir, amused by the way Salmoneus couldn't seem to keep his sandals on and run at the same time.

"Never before seen by human eyes!"

Dragar reached out to grab his shoulder, but Salmoneus skipped away, tripped, almost fell, and bowed comically at the giggles and applause that came his way.

"Ladies and gentlemen, the Salmoneus Traveling Theater of Fun proudly, and at great expense, presents . . . Dragar the Magician versus . . . the Red Power Beast!"

And with a deep breath and silent prayer, Hercules stepped into the arena.

The audience didn't quite know what to make of it when they finally saw Hercules—if this was the Red Power Beast, where was that curly red thing he wore the other night? Where was the Beast? Where was the power? Unless, of course, he really was going to break a tree over his head, thus proving that he was a lot stronger than he looked.

Salmoneus couldn't smile any longer. He looked pleadingly at Hercules and raced off the floor.

Dragar only nodded. "So."

Hercules nodded. "Yes."

"You didn't die."

"You thought I would?"

"One can but hope."

Hercules shrugged.

Dragar laid a hand on his forehead, closed his eyes briefly, and exhaled loudly, making it clear he considered this less than a petty interruption.

"You can't fight me and win, you know. You've already seen that."

Hercules felt the stiffness in his shoulder and the faint throbbing in his head. But he shrugged as if to say that not every battle wins every war.

Dragar snorted. "You think your . . . your so-called divine status will be enough to stop me?"

"Oh, yes," Hercules promised him. "Oh, yes."

Only those in the first two rows could hear the exchange, and the arena quickly filled with the sound of those passing the conversation along to the rest of the crowd.

The whispering sounded like the wind.

"With what?" Dragar wanted to know. "Your thick skull? That ridiculous shirt? Or perhaps you're counting on those clumsy bare hands?"

Hercules looked at his hands. They were indeed empty; he had left the makeshift club back in the tunnel.

You know, his inner voice said, sometimes I wonder how you made it this far.

*Idiot* was the mildest thing he called himself then, plus a few things he knew would make his mother pass out.

But aloud he answered, "Sure."

Dragar rolled his eyes in disgust and lifted the staff over his head.

Hercules took a step toward him. "One chance," he offered mildly. "One chance to change your mind, Dragar, and stop this before someone gets hurt."

Dragar bared his teeth. "Hurt? Oh, my dear Hercules, if these peasant dolts only get hurt, they'll feel blessed by the gods."

Hercules felt his chest tighten as he glanced around him at the several hundred faces turned toward him—men, women, children, all leaning forward, their expressions intense.

Then a querulous voice called from the front row, "Excuse me? Mr. Dragar? You want to repeat that, please?"

Dragar swiveled his head around and glowered.

"Only fair, you know," the voice continued. "I mean, that Beast fellow doesn't look like much, you know what I mean? Beefy, but not terribly smart. Hardly worth the money. The least you can do is speak up."

Beefy? Hercules thought; hardly worth the money?

"Like *this*?" Dragar bellowed, thunder and lightning in his voice, amplified to such a degree that a few people uttered soft screams, and a few more covered their ears.

189

The voice didn't answer; Hercules figured it belonged to the skinny guy now slumped over the wall.

"One chance," he repeated.

"Die," Dragar sneered.

And the Eye of the Ram opened.

Bolts of fiercely orange light tried to spear Hercules' chest, but the arm guards deflected them one by one into the ground.

Fireballs circled like hawks over his head, but again the arm guards scattered them into sparks. Hercules circled sideways to his left, and the bolts and fire followed; he changed direction, moving faster, ducking and dodging while the sorcerous missiles exploded against the base of the wall.

The audience finally applauded; this was more like it.

Dragar's eyes narrowed in frustration. The faster he attacked, the faster Hercules moved out of way.

Hercules, for his part, smiled mockingly, hoping the man didn't yet understand that stalling had become a major part of his plan while he figured out what the rest of it was.

Meanwhile, Dragar's impatience was Hercules' strongest ally, and he used it by skipping a few steps while, at the same time, deflecting all that the sorcerer threw at him.

Dragar growled and bared his teeth again. His arms had a difficult time holding the ram aloft, and his aim suffered for it. Now the fireballs and firebolts more often than not slammed into the cobblestones.

Hercules bowed, although he kept his head up, his gaze on Dragar's narrowed eyes.

Some of the audience tittered, recognizing in this the bumbling magician they had seen in the first show.

"One chance," Hercules offered.

Dragar snarled, and out of the Eye snaked a long purple flare that pinwheeled low, then high, then whipped past Hercules into the wall.

He grunted and stared at his upper arm.

The audience saw the blood at the same time, and most of them belatedly understood that this wasn't an act at all.

Hercules gripped his arm just below the wound, willing the pain to a place where he couldn't feel it. He barely deflected the next attack, and the attack after that.

Dragar paused, breathing heavily, frowning as he considered his next move.

At the same time there was a palpable shift in the audience's reaction; a few tried to climb over the walls in back, not wanting to take a chance on the usual exits.

Dragar raised his arms again and shouted, "No!"

The staff spun; from the Eye came a continuous flow of glaring white that ended only when Dragar brought his arms down and set the butt of the staff on the ground near his right foot, his left hand pompously on his hip.

"You will go," he said, "when I say you can go."

Hercules looked to the top of the arena and had

to tighten his jaw to keep from groaning: a slow-moving white wall surrounded the coliseum. Every few seconds a blue or red spark flared and died within it.

There was a moment when he thought the crowd would stampede, but a gesture from Dragar soon had them all seated again. And silent.

"Now," the sorcerer said, and snapped his fingers. "You wanted a Beast? You shall have him."

A figure stumbled out of the tunnel, dazed, barely able to keep his feet.

"No!" Aulma cried as she ran into the arena. "Please, no!"

Salmoneus was right behind her; he grabbed her shoulders and held on, but it took Flovi's help to stop her.

Virgil Cribus moved stiff-legged toward Dragar, but he looked at Hercules, begging for help.

Dragar stopped him with a gesture, and the Eye opened again.

White light from it formed threads, a dazzling web that covered the young man before he could move.

Then the strands fell away in pieces, each one turning to brief flame as it hit the ground.

"Now, there," Dragar said smugly, "is a Beast."

It was at least three feet high at the shoulders, with the head and mane of a black lion. The body was that of a great mountain wolf, its gleaming black pelt rippling as it padded around the outside of the arena, pointed ears laid back, its long tail hairless and thick and covered with spikes that resembled a cobra's fangs.

A steady low growl came from deep in its throat.

Its claws were so long they sounded like whip cracks against the floor each time it took a step.

When it spotted Aulma, pressed in terror against the wall, Salmoneus right beside her, it shook its huge head, tongues of fire flying from its mane.

When it spotted Hercules, it roared.

And as it roared, it charged.

# 21

There were, Hercules reckoned, a number of ways he could handle this situation.

He could run, but Dragar had stationed himself at the south tunnel, the Eye firmly in hand; and at the other end, Aulma and Salmoneus still cowered near the tunnel's mouth, too terrified to move. Besides, that would only postpone the problem, not solve it.

He could sprint around the arena's circumference in the hope that the creature would follow, get dizzy, and be too weak to resist very much when Hercules broke its fat ugly neck. That, however, depended on the assumption that Hercules was faster than the beast. And based upon the speed with which it charged, that wasn't very likely.

Giving up was out of the question.

Fighting being the only viable option left, Hercules charged the Beast himself and, at the last second, vaulted cleanly over its head, just as the immense teeth snapped at where his midsection had been.

Hercules landed lightly and whirled, arms spread; the Beast skidded to a halt and thumped easily against the wall, its spiked tail gouging furrows out of the stone.

Without looking, Hercules called, "A club, a sword!" to those still in the tunnel.

They didn't move.

"Anything!"

They still didn't move.

The Beast prowled, its head swaying side to side as it gauged the distance to Hercules' throat, its fur still rippling as if it were a living thing unto itself.

No one in the audience made a sound, or moved a muscle.

When the Beast charged again, Hercules did as well, and again he leapt over the great head and gnashing teeth.

A third time worked just as well; the fourth time, he almost tripped; the fifth time, he realized he was getting winded, and only luck prevented the Beast from snapping off his foot.

On the sixth try he noticed almost too late that the creature kept its forequarters high, the better to spring up and around, the better to try to use its forepaws to disembowel him as he passed over. Instead, Hercules darted to its right and threw himself onto its back, wrapping his arms around its neck and his legs around its chest.

The lion-beast bellowed, snapping its head frantically from side to side in a futile effort to take a piece of Hercules with each bite.

It bucked, it ran, it bucked, it stopped short and ran again—nothing worked.

But Hercules wasn't able to slow it down either. The neck was too thick and muscled for easy strangulation, and it didn't take a genius to understand that he was trapped. Letting go would throw him to the ground, and the thing would be on him before he could recover; yet staying on wouldn't last much longer, because his arms were already strained to the limit, and they would soon lose their strength. Unless his legs did first.

The Beast solved the problem for him—after spinning in a clumsy circle as fast as it could, it lost its balance and toppled onto its side. Hercules grunted as he hit the ground, and grunted again when he lashed out with his boots, catching the Beast square in its exposed belly as he rolled away.

His arms were scraped; one cheek felt as if it had been ground with a fistful of gravel. He pushed himself up, and fell immediately to one knee when his right leg gave way.

The Beast, confused for a moment when it realized its rider was gone, lifted its muzzle to the sky and roared.

Dragar laughed.

Sweat spilled into Hercules' eyes, and he wiped it away impatiently with the backs of his hands. It wasn't until he looked at his palms that he realized it wasn't sweat at all; it was blood.

It had caught him; sometime during that awful dance, it had caught him with a claw.

To make matters worse, he was more winded than

ever, and as he watched the Beast stalk him, tail high and eyes gleaming, he thought he heard someone call him from behind.

He shook his head—*Don't bother me, I'm trying not to die out here.*

The Beast charged, and stopped abruptly less than twenty feet away. It cocked its head and stared at him with one eye.

"Hercules!"

It was Aulma, and he shook his head again, sharply.

"Don't hurt him!"

That was enough to make him look over his shoulder and ask her with a single glance if she was out of her bloody mind.

She was still with Salmoneus, still crouched against the wall. One finger pointed. "Virgil," was all she could say.

Frowning, Hercules looked at the Beast, and knew with a sinking heart what she meant—if he killed this creature, he would be killing Virgil as well.

But if he let the thing live, it would kill him, and Virgil would still die, along with everyone else.

He could hear Aulma weeping; he could sense the people of Phyphe trying not to scream; he could see Dragar strutting at the mouth of the other tunnel.

With a hand on his knee he pushed himself up, shook the hair from his eyes, and swallowed the bile that had risen in his throat.

The Beast's haunches began to quiver; its tail sliced through the air; its nostrils flared as it caught the scent of its prey's blood.

Hercules lifted his hands and beckoned: *Come on, come on, let's get this over with.*

Like all good creatures that had decided on their next meal, it obliged. With a ground-shaking roar.

Hercules didn't run. He spread his legs slightly, and waited, watching, measuring, not bothering to tell himself that he had one shot, and one shot only. It was, under the circumstances, considerably more than self-evident.

At ten feet away the Beast leapt, claws out to slash, mouth open to rend and tear. But its angle was such that Hercules couldn't do something clever like duck, or leap over it, or fall down and let it sail helplessly overhead.

Hercules didn't duck, didn't fall down, didn't leap—he turned sharply and stepped back, taking the Beast's shoulder against his chest while, at the same time, bringing his right fist down on its skull. The resultant collision knocked him a good six feet through the air, and when he landed on his back his lungs forgot to work.

He wheezed, he gasped, he forced himself onto his side, and then to his hands and knees.

The Beast still stood, but it swayed, unable to get all four legs in order.

Light-headed and dizzy, Hercules staggered toward it, ignoring Dragar's scream of rage, ignoring Aulma's scream for mercy.

He stood over the Beast and said, "I'm sorry, Virgil," and brought his fist down again.

The crunch was loud enough to be heard in the t͟ ͟row.

The Beast closed its eyes and, after a long second, collapsed with a sigh.

Despite Aulma's scream of despair, Hercules turned and marched toward Dragar. "Now it's you," he said, his voice low and steady.

Dragar grinned and pointed the ram at Hercules' heart. "You've forgotten something, haven't you?"

Aulma screamed again, hoarsely, harshly.

The audience stirred as well—soft cries and whimpers and not a few muffled screams of its own.

Hercules didn't stop.

Dragar backed up, disbelieving. "You're insane, Hercules. I can kill you with a single blow."

Hercules didn't answer.

Another scream, hoarse and harsh, as Dragar lifted the staff over his head with both hands, muttered a word, and opened the Eye.

"Insane!" he yelled.

Hercules neither swerved nor flinched as he watched the silver head swing in a wide circle before it paused, trembling; he kept his gaze on Dragar's face, puffed and red with rage and madness.

"Not another step," Dragar warned, voice quivering.

"Your turn," Hercules told him.

Dragar's eyes widened, his mouth opened, and he bellowed as he brought the Eye down toward Hercules' head.

And bellowed again when something huge and dark swept out of the sky and snatched it from its hands.

"No!" he screamed, reaching toward it desperately.

Hercules hesitated, momentarily confused, until Agatra dropped the staff into his hands and flew away.

Dragar gaped, hands up in a quaking plea for mercy, clasping in prayer as he dropped to his knees.

Hercules stood over him, no expression on his face.

The arena quieted.

Hercules turned the staff over in his hands, admiring the spiral wood, the workmanship of the skull, the tingling he felt as its power ebbed and surged.

"Anything," Dragar begged, nearly weeping. "I'll give you anything you want."

Hercules nodded at the ram. "It's all in here."

"Yes. Yes, I swear it. You . . ." He stretched out a hand. "You give it back, and I'll grant you anything you want."

"I see."

Dragar's smile was obsequious and sickening. "Anything, Hercules. Anything at all."

All in here, Hercules thought; it's all in here.

He reached down with his free hand and grabbed Dragar's robe, yanked him to his feet, and dragged him to the arena's center. Then he switched his grip to the back of the man's neck, squeezing just hard enough to let the sorcerer know how easily it could be snapped.

He pointed at the fallen Beast. "Say the word,
r."

Dragar sputtered and squirmed, but lay a palsied hand on the spiral staff and whispered something Hercules didn't understand.

The white threads gathered over the Beast again, fell apart, and Virgil lay unmoving on the cobblestones as Aulma dropped to his side and cradled his head in her lap.

"The wall," Hercules said.

Another word, and the white wall vanished, letting in the wind.

"We work well together," Dragar dared to say. Then he lowered his voice: "Anything at all, remember? Anything—you just name it."

Hercules squeezed, and Dragar whimpered, hunching his shoulders and clutching at his stomach with a free hand.

Agatra settled on the ground, away from the others. She said nothing; she didn't have to.

"Peyra?" Hercules called.

A faint voice answered, "Over here."

He turned, dragging the sorcerer with him, until he spotted the young woman, pushing her way through the crowd down to the front row. He gestured, and two large men lifted her under the arms, swung her over the wall, and lowered her gently to the ground.

Hercules nodded, and she reached into her pouch.

"The word," he ordered Dragar.

It was said, and Peyra couldn't move when she saw her husband sitting at her feet, wan and thin and dazed, but plainly still alive.

*Anything,* Dragar mouthed when Hercules finally looked at him again.

In disdain Hercules shoved him away, and showed him a fist when he made to lunge for the staff. Dragar dropped instantly to his knees again, hands clasped. "You and I, Hercules, you and I. You know it, you know it."

Hercules gripped the staff with both hands, held it up, and shook his head. "It's beautiful."

"It's the most beautiful thing on this earth."

"And it's all in here, all you learned, all in here."

Dragar nodded eagerly.

"And you burned the scroll that taught you."

Again Dragar nodded. "It's . . ." He stopped, and the horror that crossed his face made Hercules smile. "No."

Hercules raised his arms, and Dragar's gaze fixed on the ram. "If you die, it would take someone a long time to learn its power, I suppose."

"You wouldn't." Dragar looked at the others one by one. "He wouldn't." He turned back. "You're Hercules. You don't kill people, I know that. I've heard the stories, I know that."

The silver ram's head rotated as Hercules turned the staff. "That's true. Most of the time." His expression hardened. "Most of the time I kill monsters."

Dragar watched the ram.

"Like you, Dragar. Like you."

Dragar threw up his hands and screamed as Hercules brought the Ram down, twisting it aside at the last moment to slam it on the ground.

* * *

There was no smoke, no fire, no rending of the air.

The Eye of the Ram shattered as if made of common clay, and the pieces rolled and bounced across the ground. Before they vanished. One by one.

Dragar wept bitterly and begged for mercy.

Agatra made her way over and looked at him with contempt. "You didn't do it," she said to Hercules.

"I did what had to be done, nothing more."

She harrumphed. "Men. Can't trust them to do anything right."

Hercules couldn't bear to look at the sniveling Dragar anymore. "Oh . . . do what you want. He's all yours, I can't abide him."

Dragar snapped his head up. "What? I'm what?"

Agatra unfolded her wings, rose slowly, and said, "I'll give you a head start." She shook her head sadly when Dragar tried to run before he'd even managed to stand. "Pathetic," she said. "It's almost too easy."

"Then don't do it," Hercules suggested. "He probably doesn't like to fly."

"Are you nuts?" she answered, and swooped after the sprinting magician, snared his shoulders with her talons, and lifted him shrieking over the wall and into the night.

# 22

It was amazing how rapidly the place emptied.

One minute the seats were full to overflowing; the next, there were only a handful of people left, too stunned to move, almost too relieved even to breathe.

Hercules pushed his hands back through his hair, and winced when they found the gash the Beast had left him. Salmoneus took his arm.

"You've saved my life again."

"It's getting to be a habit."

Salmoneus grinned. "Yeah, but you love it, don't you?"

Hercules bit back the first response that came to mind, and the second, and the third. By then, Salmoneus had begun to look a little hurt, and he couldn't help but smile despite the urge to pop him one, just for the heck of it.

Salmoneus shrugged; he understood. "Come on. I'll get you fixed up. That's a nasty wound there."

"In a minute," Hercules answered, and walked

over to Peyra and her husband, still seated at her feet. "Will he be all right?"

"I'm starving," Garus complained, and frowned. "Who are you?" He stared at his wife. "Who is this man?"

"Just a friend," Hercules answered with a smile. He leaned over and kissed Peyra's cheek. "Just a friend."

"Thank you," she whispered.

"It's all right," he told her. "It's what friends are for."

As he walked away, he heard her say something to Garus, who choked and said, "He's *who*?" And "I was a *what*?"

Hercules didn't look back. He headed straight for Aulma and Virgil, who was on his feet now and leaning heavily against her.

"My head hurts," Virgil complained, massaging it gingerly.

"He doesn't remember anything," Aulma said gratefully.

"Remember what?"

Hercules nodded. "I'm glad. But I want you to know that I pulled that last punch."

"What punch?" Virgil said.

Aulma smiled. "I know that now, and I thank you for it. I think . . . I think I'm going to find a new job." She glanced at the sky and laughed. "I guess I'll have to."

Hercules offered his hand, and she took it. "Take care of him," he said. "He has a thick skull, but a good heart."

Virgil looked around the arena, squinting as he cocked his head. "Who's ringing that damn bell?"

Aulma released the hand and took Virgil into her arms. "It's all right, dear," she whispered. "It'll go away soon."

"I hope not, it's really pretty once you get used to it."

Hercules covered his mouth with one hand to stifle the laugh there, winked at Aulma, and walked away.

It was time to go.

As always, it was time to go.

Salmoneus waited anxiously, shifting his weight from one foot to the other, gazing forlornly at the empty seats. Another dream crushed, another fortune lost.

Hercules draped an arm around the little man's shoulders, and they headed for the exit. "I'm sorry, Salmoneus. It really was a pretty good idea."

"It was dumb."

"No, it was before its time."

"You think so? You really think so?"

They looked at each other before Hercules said, "Nope, not for a minute."

Whatever retort Salmoneus had was thwarted when Flovi called them. They turned and saw the musician and Merta hurrying toward them arm in arm, their faces so suffused with joy it made Hercules, for a moment, inexplicably sad.

"Hey," Flovi said, puffing a little. "You can't go without saying good-bye."

Hercules shook his hand. "Good-bye, Flovi."

"That's it? Good-bye? That's it?"

"You want me to sing it?"

"One note," Salmoneus warned, "and I don't care who you are, I'll deck you."

Hercules mock-glared, and Salmoneus put up his fists, danced around a little, then dropped his hands and sighed. "What's the use?" he said as he walked hangdoggedly into the tunnel. "I'd only screw that up, too."

"Listen," Merta said before Hercules could go after him, "we want to thank you."

"You're welcome."

"No," Flovi said earnestly. "It's more than that, Hercules. Not only did you save my life, you also gave me a reason to live. My destiny, remember?"

Hercules nodded.

Flovi hugged Merta to him with one arm. "You heard us?"

Hercules smiled. "Beautiful. Magnificent. I take it you're going to travel on your own?"

Merta turned to Flovi, eyes shining. "We may not get rich, but we're going to have a wonderful time not doing it."

Flovi cupped her cheeks with his hands. "Ah," he said softly. "Sweet mystery of Phyphe, at last I've found you."

Merta blushed.

Hercules blushed and turned away, a wave over his shoulder when they bid him a farewell.

But they were right, he thought as he touched the caked blood on his arm and in his hair. They probably won't get rich, but they won't be poor either.

They'll sing because they love it, and because they're good at it, and the purses they'll receive will only be a bonus.

It was, in many ways, a life much like his.

And that wasn't really a bad way to live after all.

He caught up with Salmoneus outside the arena. His friend stood with slumped shoulders amid the scattered wreckage of his caravans.

"They must have done it after they left," he said, indicating the shattered walls and smashed roof, the wheels crushed, the spokes ripped away. "I guess this really is the end of the Traveling Theater of Fun."

Hercules didn't know quite what to say. Other schemes had gone bust, but he'd never seen his friend quite so depressed. He took Salmoneus' arm and turned him toward town. "Tell you what—we'll go back to the inn, fix my head, get something to eat, something to drink, get a good night's sleep, and leave first thing in the morning."

"And go where?" Salmoneus said wearily.

Hercules shrugged. "What does it matter? We'll have a good time no matter what, don't you think?"

Salmoneus sighed loudly and lowered his head, sighed again. "I suppose."

"What's his problem?" a rasping voice demanded.

"Post-bad-guy-gets-his blues," he said as Agatra landed in front of them. Salmoneus didn't even jump.

Agatra tsked derisively.

"Speaking of which," Hercules said, looking around and not finding Dragar.

"Oh," the Harpy said. "Him." She lifted one claw and flexed the talons. "Not as young as I used to be, you know. I figured to take him where he wouldn't do anyone anymore harm, got over those bad rapids above the waterfall and . . ." Her wings rose and fell in a shrug. "Oops."

"Oops?"

She shrugged again. "Life's a bitch and then you fall," she said. "An old Harpy saying."

"Well, look, I'm kind of glad you're back before I left. I, uh, wanted to thank you for . . ." He gestured vaguely toward the forest. "You know."

"Yeah, well . . ." She clawed the ground a little. "Thing is, you see, you're one of them demigod things, so you're not properly a man. So I guess I wanted to kind of . . . you know . . . for the . . . you know . . . back then in the . . . you know."

"I know."

She sniffed, and rubbed the side of her nose briskly. "Good. Just so you know."

Salmoneus put his hands on his hips. "Do you two have any idea what you're talking about?"

"Sure," they said.

Salmoneus sighed. "That figures."

Agatra cleared her throat, bobbed her head, and after a moment's awkward hesitation, said, "Well, look, if you're ever around Nevila, you can drop in if you want. I probably won't kill you."

"Thank you," Hercules answered solemnly. "I'll do that. It's a promise."

Agatra nodded.

He nodded.

Salmoneus sighed.

And in the dark behind the Harpy there came a soft and plaintive quacking.

Agatra took to the air immediately, circled once, and shot northward over the arena. Right behind, a large white blur followed, keeping pace without half trying.

Hercules laughed. "A duck, a Harpy, and unrequited love. Sounds like one of Flovi's songs, don't you think?"

Salmoneus didn't answer; he just stared openmouthed.

Hercules shook his shoulder. "Salmoneus, are you all right?"

Salmoneus only blinked.

Hercules backed away. "No," he said, holding up his hands. "We haven't even had dinner yet."

Salmoneus raised a thoughtful finger as he headed toward the town. "It might work, you know?"

Hercules hurried after him. "Salmoneus," he warned.

Salmoneus drew a sketch in the air. "A leather bag, maybe, or a tube."

"Salmoneus!"

"You write a letter, you stick it in the tube, you put it in the duck's beak—"

"Dammit, Salmoneus!"

Salmoneus stopped and turned. "Of course, if he quacks, the tube will drop." He beamed. "But not to worry, I'll figure it out." He took Hercules' arm.

"I tell you, friend, we're going to make a fortune."

Hercules couldn't help himself: "We?"

"Well, somebody has to pay for them. And the training, right? I sure don't have any spare dinars, and you know it was your fault that the Traveling Theater died tonight, all that fighting and stuff. Don't you feel the least bit guilty?"

Sure, Hercules thought—about keeping you alive all these years.

"Oh, don't be so gloomy, Hercules. After all," Salmoneus said slyly, "didn't you just tell me we'll have a good time no matter what we do?"

Hercules knew there was a phrase for that; he couldn't remember it, but it meant that he had just been hanged by his own words.

"The Salmoneus Messenger Service, what do you think?"

And the man was right—the battle was over, time to find a new challenge.

"The Hercules Carrier Ducks."

Or, Hercules thought as he laughed, it was high time he found that cave.

But never boring, thank the gods.

Never boring at all.

# WARRIOR PRINCESS™

__**THE EMPTY THRONE**         1-57297-200-9/$5.99

In a small village, Xena and her protégé, Gabrielle, discover that all the men in town have disappeared without a trace. They must uncover the truth before they too disappear...

A novel by Ru Emerson based on the Universal television series created by John Schulian and Robert Tapert

__**THE HUNTRESS AND THE SPHINX**

                                  1-57297-215-7/$5.99

No one is braver or faster than the legendary huntress, Atalanta. Or so she says. When Xena and Gabrielle are asked to rescue a group of kidnapped children, Atalanta is the first to volunteer, after all she is the strongest. But when they find the kidnapper, Xena realizes that no one is strong enough to defeat the deadly riddles of the legendary Sphinx...

A novel by Ru Emerson based on the Universal television series created by John Schulian and Robert Tapert

***Coming in March '97: THE THIEF OF HERMES***

VISIT THE PUTNAM BERKLEY BOOKSTORE CAFÉ ON THE INTERNET:
http://www.berkley.com/berkley

Payable in U.S. funds. No cash accepted. Postage & handling: $1.75 for one book, 75¢ for each additional. Maximum postage $5.50. Prices, postage and handling charges may change without notice. Visa, Amex, MasterCard call 1-800-788-6262, ext. 1, or fax 1-201-933-2316; refer to ad # 693

Or, check above books   **Bill my:** ☐ Visa ☐ MasterCard ☐ Amex _____ (expires)
and send this order form to:
The Berkley Publishing Group  Card#_____

P.O. Box 12289, Dept. B   Daytime   Phone#_____ ($10 minimum)
Newark, NJ 07101-5289   Signature_____

Please allow 4-6 weeks for delivery. **Or enclosed is my:** ☐ check ☐ money order
Foreign and Canadian delivery 8-12 weeks.

**Ship to:**

| | | |
|---|---|---|
| Name_____ | Book    Total | $_____ |
| Address_____ | Applicable  Sales  Tax (NY, NJ, PA, CA, GST Can.) | $_____ |
| City_____ | Postage   &   Handling | $_____ |
| State/ZIP_____ | Total  Amount  Due | $_____ |

**Bill to:**      Name_____
Address_____City_____
State/ZIP_____